Born in Essex in 1964, Ross Kemp is best known for his portrayal of Grant Mitchell in *EastEnders*. His father was a senior detective with the Metropolitan Police force, and as a result crime has always fascinated Kemp. In 2007 *Ross Kemp on Gangs* won a BAFTA for Best Factual Series.

Also available:

Ganglands: Brazil

PENGUIN BOOKS

PENGUIN BOOKS

Published by the Penguin Group
Penguin Books Ltd, 80 Strand, London WC2R 0RL, England
Penguin Group (USA) Inc., 375 Hudson Street, New York, New York 10014, USA
Penguin Group (Canada), 90 Eglinton Avenue East, Suite 700, Toronto, Ontario, Canada M4P 2Y3
(a division of Pearson Penguin Canada Inc.)
Penguin Ireland, 25 St Stephen's Green, Dublin 2, Ireland (a division of Penguin Books Ltd)
Penguin Group (Australia), 250 Camberwell Road, Camberwell, Victoria 3124, Australia
(a division of Pearson Australia Group Pty Ltd)
Penguin Books India Pvt Ltd, 11 Community Centre, Panchsheel Park, New Delhi – 110 017, India
Penguin Group (NZ), 67 Apollo Drive, Rosedale, North Shore 0632, New Zealand
(a division of Pearson New Zealand Ltd)
Penguin Books (South Africa) (Pty) Ltd, 24 Sturdee Avenue, Rosebank, Johannesburg 2196, South Africa

Penguin Books Ltd, Registered Offices: 80 Strand, London WC2R 0RL, England

penguin.com

First published 2010
1

Set in Garamond MT 13/15.25pt
Typeset by Palimpsest Book Production Limited, Falkirk, Stirlingshire
Made and printed in England by Clays Ltd, St Ives plc

British Library Cataloguing in Publication Data
A CIP catalogue record for this book is available from the British Library

ISBN: 978–0–141–32590–3

www.greenpenguin.co.uk

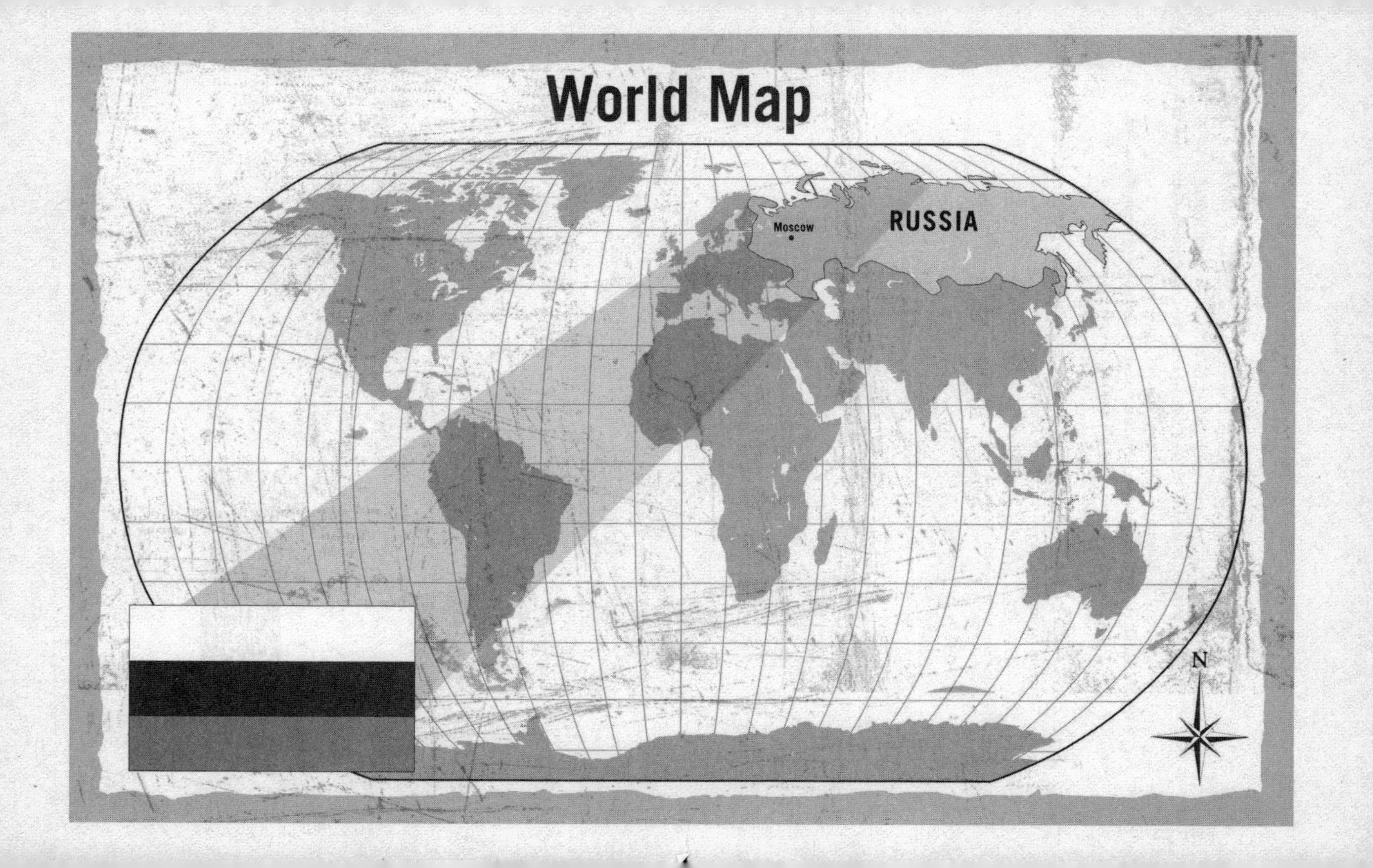
World Map
RUSSIA
Moscow
N

1. Hate Crimes

20 April: 2045 hours.

Lena Saroyan hurries through Mayakovskaya metro station, her trainers squeaking softly on the tiled floor. At this time of night, the station is relatively quiet, the breathless crowds that press the Moscow underground during rush hour having thinned to a trickle of commuters. Even so, there had been a lengthy queue at the ticket booth, and Lena is running late as it is.

Even as she rushes, she can't help but admire her surroundings. Lena has been living in Moscow for only three weeks, and the labyrinthine underground system still makes her as wide-eyed as a child – especially Mayakovskaya, with its colonnaded central hall, resplendent in white and black marble and pink rhodonite, and high vaulted ceilings inlaid with mosaics. Every time Lena travels down the long, snaking escalators, it feels as though she is travelling to the very centre of the earth.

At the bottom of the escalator, a male announcer in a glass booth openly stares at Lena as she walks past him. Lena barely notices. Even though she is only seventeen, she has already learned to ignore men's reactions to her presence; the leering smiles and the wolf-whistles that follow her as she walks down the street. For this, she has her Armenian mother to thank – or to blame: anyone who has seen the two women together knows the source of Lena's slender figure, her raven-black hair and her beautiful, feline features.

It had also been her mother who had persuaded Lena to enter a modelling competition back home in Volgograd – an industrial city in southern Russia. *Just a bit of harmless fun*, she had argued lightly, *besides, you might even enjoy yourself.* And Lena *had* enjoyed herself, once she had got over her nerves at parading up and down in front of strangers. Not only that, but she had won, earning herself a six-month contract with an agency in the capital. Which was how Lena had found herself spending the afternoon in a run-down photographer's studio in the Presnya district of Moscow, modelling summer dresses for a catalogue. Not exactly the Paris fashion show, Lena thinks to herself ruefully, but as Alexei had pointed out, it was all good experience.

At the thought of her boyfriend, Lena smiles. Alexei had insisted on coming with her to Moscow, arguing that he could enrol on an engineering course at the city's State University in the autumn. Although she was too proud to admit it, secretly Lena had been hoping that's what he would do. Moscow was a large place to have no friends in, and she always felt safe around Alexei. Only he seemed able to calm her wilful temper – a trait as strong in Lena's Russian father as beauty was in her mother. In private, Alexei teases her about it, jokingly calls her an angry bear. No one else could get away with that.

Lena checks her watch, stifling a squeak of exasperation. Alexei's fight was going to start any minute now, and she wouldn't be there at ringside to support him. It was the wretched photographer's fault – he hadn't been happy with the shoot, and Lena had had to sit there, inwardly seething, as he fussily fiddled with her dress and the lighting. Still, at least he had kept his hands to himself. Even after only three weeks, Lena has already heard enough cautionary tales from other models to keep an eye out for photographers' wandering hands.

She hurries along the central hall, the grand architecture illuminated by rings of electric lights above her head. The serene atmosphere suddenly reminds her of the church she used to go to back in Volgograd, a thought that gives her an unexpected pang of homesickness. Lena decides to call her parents after she has caught up with Alexei. *If* she ever manages to get to the gym . . .

Thankfully, a train pulls up just as Lena arrives on the platform. The carriage is half empty: a handful of office workers who must have been working late, and late-night shoppers laden with bags. Lena sits down opposite an elderly Tajik man with a long white beard that is bright against his weathered skin. He waits patiently for the train to move off, his hands clasped in his lap. Lena pulls out a magazine from her bag and flicks through photos of actors and celebrities, idly wondering whether one day she will open up a magazine and find a picture of herself staring back.

As the train continues north along the Green Line, stop-by-stop passengers slowly begin to drain from the carriage. Wearied by her long day in front of the camera, and the lullaby rocking motion of the train, Lena puts down her magazine. Her eyelids droop shut.

Then, as the carriage doors open at Sokol station, everything changes.

Lena smells the men before she sees them: a thick mixture of cigarettes, alcohol and body odour. At once wide awake, she glances up to see two young men barge on to the train. The first is muscular and bull-headed, his shaved scalp gleaming in the carriage lights. He wears a leather jacket over a T-shirt and combat trousers, an air of sullen menace hanging off him like deodorant. The second is a teenager, less heavy-set, his young face topped with short blond hair. A tattoo of a dragon rises up from above his collar and writhes around his neck. He drunkenly surveys the carriage, a look of disgust in his eyes, then raises his right arm in salute and shouts out: '*Sieg Heil!*'

No one responds. The teenager notices Lena looking at them and elbows the other, making a lewd gesture about her breasts. The giant skinhead sniggers.

'Hey, baby,' he calls out to Lena. 'You like what you see? You want to spend time with a real Russian man?' He grabs his crotch, laughing.

Lena looks down at her magazine, trying to ignore him. This isn't the first time this sort of thing has happened to her. It was typical, though: of all the carriages in Moscow, she has to pick the one with these assholes in it.

'Don't play hard to get,' the blond-haired one says cajolingly. 'The Eagles know how to treat a lady. We'll make sure you're satisfied.'

Opposite Lena, the elderly Tajik man shakes his head and makes a small sound of disapproval. The teenager looks at him sharply.

'What did you say to me, you piece of shit?'

The Tajik says nothing, only shakes his head again.

'I asked you a question,' the boy said, through clenched teeth. 'Don't you speak Russian?'

Lena realizes that she is holding her breath.

Instead of replying, the Tajik man rises slowly to his feet and moves to find another seat in the carriage. The bull-headed man runs over to him and grabs his arm, unleashing a furious barrage of punches. The older man tries to cover himself with his arms, but it is no protection from the clubbing blows raining down upon him – he collapses back on to the seat. With a whoop, the teenager leaps on to the seat next to him and begins kicking him in the head.

For a few seconds, the other passengers are too shocked to react. But as the violence continues, a middle-aged woman hurriedly collects her bags and goes over to the other side of the carriage; a teenage boy buries his head in a book and refuses to look up. No one wants to get involved. As the Tajik crumples to the floor of the train, Lena stands up, indignation coursing through her veins.

'Stop it!' she shouts. 'Leave him alone!'

'Who asked you, bitch?' the skinhead spits. 'Stay out of it!'

A voice at the back of Lena's head – her mother's – is urging her to walk away, to protect herself. But at that moment, Lena is her father's daughter. Righteous anger takes over.

'Oh, you're real heroes, aren't you?' she says sarcastically. 'It takes two of you to beat up a harmless old man!'

The blond teenager strides over to Lena, drenching her in the smell of beer. She forces herself not to back down as he sticks his face so close to hers that their noses almost touch.

'You're not pure Russian either, are you?' he hisses. 'Typical of you mongrels to stick together.'

'If you're the best that "pure Russia" has to offer,' retorts Lena, 'I'd rather be a mongrel.'

The boy nods slowly, an amused smile creeping over his face. He turns as if to walk away, then wheels back and gives Lena a shuddering backhanded slap across the face. Her head snaps back, her cheek on fire. Before she can react, he punches her, sending her sprawling to the floor by the carriage door.

The carriage swims in front of her eyes. Dimly, Lena realizes that her nose is bleeding, and that she is not going to see Alexei tonight after all. The blond teenager laughs.

'Don't look so clever now, do you?'

The bull-headed man shoves him out of the way, his face contorted with rage.

'Think you're better than us, you mongrel bitch?' he snarls. 'I'll show you who's in charge!'

The last thing Lena sees is the giant skinhead standing over her, his fist drawn back, then his arm comes down and everything goes black.

2. Round One

As the bell rang for the first round, Alexei realized that he was in deep trouble.

His opponent came charging out of his corner, catching Alexei off guard with the ferocity of his attack. The other boy was a few centimetres taller than Alexei, and he knew how to make his extra reach tell, moving in behind a series of powerful jabs. Alexei had spent half of his sixteen years learning to kickbox – spending hour after hour sweating in the gym, working the bags, trading punches and kicks inside the ring. He'd never been in better shape. And still he knew, as he backed away towards the ropes, that it wasn't going to count for anything tonight.

As the two fighters traded blows with one another, there were shouts of encouragement from the meagre audience. Although rows of chairs had been laid out across the gym, a match between two local kickboxing clubs hadn't proved much of a draw. Friends and family, mostly, and Alexei was a long way from the majority of his. Only his uncle and Lena were with him in Moscow, and Stepan was visiting an old friend that evening.

Concentrate, Alexei! he urged himself. The sheer aggression of his opponent was forcing him on to the back foot. Alexei's plan had been to stay calm and wait for his opponent to over-commit, but that seemed impossible with the other boy swarming all over him, snarls of effort emanating from behind his mouthguard with every punch.

Struggling to defend against a vicious body shot, Alexei never saw the roundhouse kick coming, only felt the impact as it rattled his skull. As he shook his head to try and clear the fog from his mind, Alexei saw his trainer, Ruslan, wince in his corner. Sensing an opening, Alexei's opponent redoubled his attack, his punches carrying even greater weight now. Alexei tried to bob and weave out of the way, but it felt as though every movement set him on a collision course with his opponent's fists. Even though they had only been fighting for a minute or so, Alexei found himself desperately wanting the bell to ring and the round to end.

He tried to throw a couple of punches back, but they were wild swings. His defence was unravelling, he knew. Another kick caught him in the side, and it became difficult to breathe. As a thumping right connected with Alexei's jaw, he felt his world begin to spin, and then suddenly the referee was standing between them, waving his arms. The bell rang, and Alexei's opponent strode back to his corner with his arms aloft. Dazed, Alexei allowed the referee to check him for signs of concussion, before walking slowly back to his corner. Ruslan gave him a consolation pat on the back, and removed Alexei's mouthguard.

'Tough fight.'

'No shit,' replied Alexei. 'You weren't the one getting hit.'

His trainer barked with laughter. 'OK, so you took a beating tonight. You'll be back. Might even land a punch next time.'

Alexei touched a tender part of his face, wincing. 'What happened, Ruslan?' he asked despairingly. 'I've been training harder than ever. Why did I just get my head kicked in?'

Ruslan scratched the stubble on his cheek. 'What do you want me to tell you? You're a nice boy, I wish I had more like you. You train hard, you have a good technique, but you lack . . .' The trainer tailed off, searching for the right word. He banged his chest over his heart. 'Fire. That boy you fought tonight, he wanted to kill you. You?' Ruslan shrugged. 'You just want a good fight. No fire.'

'That's all you've got for me?' Alexei said, with a sideways glance. 'I haven't got enough *fire*?'

Ruslan nodded. 'And use your uppercut more. When you throw that punch, Alexei, it's a thing of rare beauty. And I've seen a few in my time.'

As he stepped down from the ring apron, Alexei shielded his eyes from the glare of the lights and looked out over the sparse crowd. The girl he was looking for wasn't in her usual position in the back row. Lena didn't enjoy watching him fight, Alexei knew, even when he won, but she turned up anyway because she knew that it mattered to him. It was one of the reasons he loved her.

Ruslan followed his gaze.

'Looking for someone?'

'My girlfriend,' replied Alexei. 'She was supposed to be watching me tonight.'

'Maybe it was better for you she didn't turn up,' the trainer guffawed, slapping Alexei on the back. 'She sees that fight, maybe she goes home with the other guy.'

'Thanks, Ruslan,' Alexei said sourly.

He walked moodily back to the changing rooms and showered, the cascade of warm water soothing his aching limbs. Afterwards, checking his reflection in the mirror, Alexei saw that his face was puffy and red – he'd be sporting some impressive bruises by morning.

He was towelling his hair dry when he heard his mobile ringing: probably Lena complaining that her feet were sore from wearing high heels, Alexei grumbled to himself, or some other great modelling trauma. But when he dug his phone out of his kitbag, he saw that the number was withheld.

'Hello?' he said, frowning.

'Alexei?' Not Lena. A man's voice – a Westerner. 'Alexei Zhukov?'

'Yes. Who is this?'

'Do you speak English, Alexei?'

'A little,' Alexei said cautiously. 'Who is this?'

'My name doesn't matter right now,' the man replied. 'You need to go to the hospital in Presnya immediately. Someone you care about has been badly hurt.'

With a lurch to his stomach, Alexei thought back to the empty chair at ringside. 'Not Lena?'

'Just go to the hospital, son. We'll speak again afterwards.'

'Wait!' Alexei cried. 'How do you know all this? Who are you?'

There was a pause on the other end of the phone. 'Consider me a friend,' the man said finally, and then ended the call.

Alexei hurriedly stuffed the rest of his things into his kitbag and raced out of the locker room. On the way out, he knocked into his trainer – Ruslan shouted something after him, but Alexei didn't stop to apologize. He crashed out through the doors and on to the street.

The hospital in Presnya wasn't far from the kickboxing gym, but Alexei wasn't going to waste a second. He hailed a passing cab and leaped in the back. As the car negotiated the late-evening traffic, Alexei prayed that the phone call had been some kind of sick practical joke. He'd turn up at the hospital and make a fool of himself by frantically asking for someone who wasn't there, but it would be all right, because as long as Lena was OK Alexei didn't care what happened. *God, please let it be a joke*, he thought to himself.

The hospital was an imposing modern building set back from the road. As the taxi pulled up outside the entrance, Alexei stuffed a ten-rouble note into the driver's hand and scrambled out. Running at full pelt through the automatic doors, Alexei nearly crashed into the reception desk. A nurse looked up from her computer with surprise.

'Yes?'

'I'm looking for my girlfriend,' Alexei panted. 'Lena Saroyan. Is she here?'

'One moment.' The nurse tapped the computer keys as she checked her records. 'She's in surgery right now.'

'Surgery?'

'I'll get a doctor to come and explain everything to you,' the nurse replied. 'In the meantime, if you could please wait over there.'

She pointed to the waiting room, where a handful of relatives were sitting expectantly for news of their loved ones, their faces drawn and pale in the weak strip-lighting. They kept glancing warily back to the other side of the waiting room, where an imposing black man was sitting on his own, his arms folded. Alexei paced across the floor, trying to ignore the horrible thoughts about Lena his mind was conjuring up. As he muttered to himself, he became aware that the black man was watching him with a coolly impassive gaze. Annoyed by the scrutiny, Alexei was about to confront him when a doctor appeared and drew him to one side.

'What's going on?' asked Alexei. 'What's happened to Lena?'

'Your girlfriend was attacked on a metro train this evening.'

'Attacked?' echoed Alexei. 'What . . . what do you mean, attacked?'

'A gang of youths beat her up – very badly, I'm afraid to say. Lena sustained some internal injuries that demanded we operated on her immediately.'

'How is she now?'

'We've staunched the internal bleeding, but she also

suffered severe head trauma.' The doctor paused. 'Lena's in a coma right now.'

'But she'll wake up, right?' Alexei said desperately.

'There's no way we can predict anything at the moment,' the doctor said sympathetically. 'For the time being, she's stable. Would you like to see her?'

Alexei nodded. Numbly, he felt the doctor take his arm and lead him through the hospital to a small room on the third floor. Nothing could have prepared Alexei for the scene within: his girlfriend stretched out on a bed, her eyes closed, her body hooked up to a mass of machines via a complicated system of tubes. A heart monitor bleeped monotonously in the silence. Seeing Lena lying there, Alexei was overwhelmed by emotion: grief at the bruises covering the girl's face, and an icy rage for the people who had inflicted them upon her. Trying to fight back the tears, he sat next to Lena's side and gently held her hand.

Alexei had no idea how long they sat together in that tiny room. Eventually the doctor returned, and told him in a low voice that he had to leave Lena until the morning. Reluctantly, Alexei let go of his girlfriend's hand and left the room.

In the corridor outside, he was surprised to see the black man from the waiting room standing by a water cooler, his hands folded behind his back. The man nodded at him.

'How is she?' he asked.

'What the hell is it to you?' snapped Alexei.

The man seemed unfazed by his reply. 'Dark times require friends,' he said, in a deep American baritone.

Something clicked in Alexei's head.

'It was you!' he exclaimed. 'You're the guy who phoned me!'

The American extended a hand. 'Allow me to introduce myself: I'm Darius Jordan, head of Trojan Industries. We have a lot to talk about, Alexei.'

3. Recruitment Drive

Alexei stared at the man's outstretched hand.

'What do you mean, we have a lot to talk about?'

Jordan glanced around the hospital corridor. 'This isn't the best place to discuss business. Why don't you take a walk with me?'

'Why don't you get the hell out of my face?' snapped Alexei, reddening with anger. 'What's it got to do with you, anyway?'

There was a polite cough behind him. Alexei turned round to see a bespectacled man in green surgical scrubs politely interject himself between Alexei and the American. 'Mr Jordan?'

'Mr Karpin.' Jordan shook the man briskly by the hand. 'I hear that the surgery went well.'

'As well as can be expected, given the circumstances. The patient is lucky that you are paying for her treatment. The facilities here are among the best in Russia.'

'The surgeons too, I hear.'

The bespectacled man smiled. 'Very kind of you to say so. I have another case to attend to now – but be assured we'll be doing everything we can for Lena.'

The man walked away, leaving Alexei in a state of

complete confusion. Why had a complete stranger paid for Lena's treatment?

'I'm not rich, you know,' he confessed to Jordan. 'I don't know if I can pay you back.'

'Not monetarily. This place doesn't come cheap, let me assure you. But maybe there's other ways we can work together. If you'll come and discuss it with me . . .'

'Talk here or not at all,' Alexei insisted. 'I'm not leaving Lena alone.'

'I understand completely,' the American replied, unruffled. 'Perhaps you'd be better off not knowing after all. I'm sorry to have troubled you.'

He turned to walk away.

'Wait!'

Jordan stopped and looked back, his eyebrow raised quizzically.

'I'd be "better off not knowing" what?' asked Alexei.

'Trojan has certain information about what happened to Lena that I thought you might want to hear. Information you might not get from the authorities.'

Alexei's eyes narrowed. 'Then how do you know about it?'

'It's my job to know these sorts of things. Listen, Alexei, I know it's difficult to take everything in right now. I wish this dreadful thing hadn't happened to Lena, and that you and I hadn't had to meet in these circumstances. All I'm offering you is a chance to understand what's going on. The rest is entirely up to you.'

'And if I don't come with you, what happens to Lena?'

Jordan spread out his palms. 'I'm a businessman,

Alexei,' he said. 'As long as Trojan Industries has a reason to be in Moscow, I can take care of Lena. But if we can't do business, then that's a different matter.'

Jordan turned on his heel and strode away, not waiting to see if Alexei followed him. Alexei glanced back at Lena through the shuttered window of her room, then jogged down the corridor after the tall American. Jordan didn't acknowledge him when Alexei caught up – something about the man's manner suggested he was used to people obeying him. They walked in silence back down to the main entrance.

Outside the hospital, Alexei zipped up his tracksuit and pulled his hood over his head. The thick winter snows might have melted away, but there was still an icy sharpness to the night air. A large black people carrier with tinted windows was parked next to the loading bay. Jordan opened the rear passenger door and gestured for Alexei to climb inside. Alexei hesitated, his simmering anger tempered by the first gnawings of fear.

The American noted the pensive look on Alexei's face. 'Don't be nervous, son,' he said. 'The safest place to be is right by my side.'

He spoke with a no-nonsense briskness that Alexei found reassuring. He climbed inside the people carrier and settled into the back seat. Two other people were sharing the vehicle's gloomy interior: a man in the driver's seat, softly drumming his fingers on the steering wheel; beside him, a woman smoked idly out of the passenger window. Neither of them said a word to Alexei as Jordan joined him in the back seat.

'Take us for a drive, Richard,' the American said crisply as he closed the door behind him. 'Nice and easy – I don't want any unnecessary attention.'

The man in the driver's seat nodded, flicked on the people carrier's headlights, and nudged the vehicle out into the traffic. As the car ploughed on through the dark streets, Darius turned to Alexei.

'You'll have to forgive my caution,' he said, 'but I prefer to talk business in a secure environment.'

'I don't know why you keep talking about business,' Alexei said stubbornly. 'All I care about is what happened to Lena.'

'It's all business, Alexei, one way or another. But OK. The police are still collecting reports on the attack tonight, but our man on the inside has had a chance to review the CCTV footage from Sokol station. The pictures aren't clear enough to make any positive identifications, but we're convinced that your girlfriend was attacked by a skinhead gang called the Moscow Eagle 88s.'

'Skinheads?' Alexei echoed incredulously. 'Why would they attack Lena?'

Darius Jordan glanced out of the window. 'I wish I could give you a proper reason, son, but it looks like a simple case of wrong place, wrong time. Today's April the twentieth – skinheads like the Eagles often go looking for targets on this day.'

'What's so special about April the twentieth?'

'It's Hitler's birthday,' the woman in the front seat said, her voice deathly cold.

Alexei listened in dumb shock as Jordan continued:

'Seems your girlfriend stepped in when these thugs started beating up a Tajik on the metro. Compared to Lena, the old guy got off lightly – he'll be out of hospital within the next few days. Owes his life to your girlfriend.'

'Typical Lena,' Alexei said faintly. 'She never walks away from a fight.'

'She sounds like quite a girl. The worst things always happen to the best people. Don't know why the world has to work like that, but it does.'

Alexei frowned. 'But how do I know that this is true? How come you can get hold of this information so quickly?'

'Contacts,' Jordan said simply. 'By now you might have guessed that Trojan Industries isn't like other businesses, Alexei. We're not interested in selling products or making money or anything like that.'

'So what are you interested in?'

Jordan's eyes glinted in the darkness. 'Gangs,' he said. 'Trojan is a shell, a front for a covert military operation. Under its auspices, we travel from country to country trying to break up the world's most violent gangs. Three months ago, we had our first successful operation in Brazil. We came to Russia because of the Moscow Eagles – our sources here have been tracking them for quite some time. Even by neo-Nazi standards, they're a brutal bunch. Now we have the perfect opportunity to take them down. Look at this.'

Opening up a slim briefcase, Jordan produced a copy of the *Moscow Times*, the city's English-language newspaper, and passed it to Alexei. On the front page, a photograph showed an angry-looking skinhead in handcuffs being marched through a crowd by a policeman.

'Recognize this man?'

Alexei shook his head.

'His name is Nikolai Borovsky. He's a member of the Moscow Eagles. He's currently on trial for the murder of two Azerbaijani workmen last August. The verdict's in tomorrow – and it looks like he's going to jail for a long time.'

'OK,' Alexei said slowly. 'But what's this got to do with me?'

'Borovsky is the Eagles' main enforcer – losing him is a massive blow to their organization. Right now, they're vulnerable to infiltration. Trojan needs an agent to gain the gang's confidence and gather enough evidence to enable us to smash the 88s for good.'

Slowly, the pieces began to fall into place in Alexei's head. 'Are you saying you want *me* to do this?'

'That's exactly what I'm saying, Alexei. Be under no illusions: this is a dangerous assignment. The Eagles are a violent and unpredictable outfit, and if you get into trouble I can't guarantee that we can help you. Trojan is a black-ops organization – if the Russian authorities find out about us, it will be an international scandal. It would spell the end for us.'

'This is crazy!' exclaimed Alexei. 'I'm not a spy! I can't do this!'

'I think you underestimate yourself,' Jordan said calmly. Returning to his briefcase, he pulled out a brown file and began flicking through it. 'Alexei Zhukov,' he read out, pursing his lips. 'Judging by his school records, he's an exemplary student. Shows particular promise in the sciences – potential to study engineering at university. Outside of school, he's a trained kickboxer who's competed at state level.'

'An all-round high achiever,' remarked the driver drily. 'I hated kids like that when I was at school.'

'It's not that surprising, Richard,' Jordan replied. 'Not when you look at his family. His grandfather, his uncle *and* his father can all boast distinguished military service for the Red Army.'

'The boy's got heroism in the genes,' the driver agreed.

Jordan snapped the file shut. When he spoke again, any trace of lightness had disappeared from his voice. 'In short, Alexei – you're a perfect candidate for Trojan Industries.'

As the car pulled up to a set of traffic lights, Alexei stared out of the window at the night sky. 'This is too much,' he said quietly. 'First Lena, now this spy stuff . . . I can't deal with it.'

'You have my sympathy, son. But we can't pick and choose our moments to fight, and Trojan needs your help. We have to make sure that what happened to Lena doesn't happen to anyone else.'

Alexei shook his head. The shock of the night's events had suddenly hit him like a brick wall. He was worried he was going to burst into tears. Seeing the distress on his face, Jordan returned the file to his briefcase saying, 'Why don't you sleep on it, and get back to us?'

The American opened his wallet and handed Alexei a

business card. 'You can contact me on that number any time, day or night. Whatever you decide to do, I need to hear from you in the next twenty-four hours. Time is of the essence.'

Alexei slipped the card into his back pocket. 'Can you let me out here, please?' he asked wearily.

The driver glanced round in surprise. 'You don't want us to take you back to the hospital?'

'Just stop the damn car!' Alexei shouted.

The driver hurriedly pulled over to the side of the road. Before Jordan could say anything else, Alexei yanked open the door and leaped out, running away down the street. He had no idea where he was running to – all he knew was that he had to put distance between himself and the American. Risking a look back over his shoulder, he was relieved to see the people carrier turning round and heading away in the opposite direction. As Alexei sprinted around the street corner, the car dimmed its headlights, disappearing into the night.

4. Courting Trouble

The next morning, in a courthouse in the Arbat district of Moscow, Rozalina Petrova nervously awaits the return of the jury. A human rights lawyer who specializes in racist attacks, she has been in this situation countless times before. Usually she keeps her emotions under control; quietly celebrating her victories, resolute in her defeats. This case, however, is different.

The defendant, Nikolai Borovsky, stands quietly in a metal cage in the centre of the courtroom: a towering man in a prison jumpsuit. As Rozalina watches him, he carefully runs a hand across the top of his bald head, mapping out the slight bumps and depressions of his skull. Rozalina doesn't scare easily – she couldn't do her job if she did – but there is something about Borovsky that chills her to the core. During her prosecution speech, he leaned against the bars, a dreamy half-smile playing on his lips. She doubts he heard a word she said.

It's the lack of emotion that bothers Rozalina. After all, she has seen the photographs of the two men Borovsky killed, their bodies dumped at the bottom of an empty and abandoned swimming pool, staining the

...acked tiles with their blood. The Azerbaijani immigrants had been so badly beaten that their corpses could only be identified by their fingerprints. Apparently Borovsky hadn't shown the slightest surprise when the police had come to arrest him – Rozalina has the nasty suspicion that he is pleased to be associated with this crime, and his 'not guilty' plea at the trial's outset was the work of his defence lawyer.

She is surprised that this one case has affected her so much. Ten years of campaigning for justice for victims of racist attacks has hardened Rozalina to the hazards that accompany her work: the hate mail, the graffiti daubed on her car, the threatening phone calls. Every time she speaks to her parents on the phone, they beg her to take up other kinds of cases. Although it breaks her heart to cause them so much worry, she has a stubborn streak that runs as deep through her soul as a Pacific trench, and this is something she's willing to risk her life for.

There is a stir in the courtroom as the jury files back in. Rozalina stands, her heart racing as the judge asks the foreman for his verdict.

'Guilty,' he replies.

Rozalina feels a small surge of triumph; unconsciously, her fist clenches. A murmur of excitement ripples through the room. Someone shouts 'Rot in hell, you bastard!' from the gallery – a relative of one of the victims. The skinhead barely seems to register the verdict. As he is led away from his cage, Borovsky searches out Rozalina and smiles at her. Then, lifting up his manacled hands, he draws an invisible dagger across his throat. A policeman manhandles him away, but Borovsky's laughter echoes in Rozalina's head long after he has vanished into the bowels of the courthouse.

People line up to shake her hand; Rozalina smiles politely and accepts their congratulations, but all she wants to do is get into her car and return to her flat. Borovsky has unsettled her more than she cares to admit. She quickly packs up her briefcase and leaves the courtroom.

A crowd has gathered on the steps outside, a volatile mixture of reporters waving microphones, protesters brandishing anti-Nazi placards, and a knot of skinheads chanting and making fascist salutes. Steeling herself for the crush, Rozalina clutches her briefcase close to her chest and tries to thread her way through the crowd. A thin line of policemen struggles to clear a path for her, buffeted on both sides. The air is thick with cheers and boos and the threat of violence. As Rozalina forges down the steps, she is assailed by different sections of the crowd:

'Miss Petrova, what are your thoughts about this conviction?'

'Death to the fascists!'

'Nikolai was a Russian hero, you bitch!'

From out of the crowd, a tattooed face twisted with hatred appears. The skinhead spits at Rozalina; she flinches as a policeman steps in, pushing the man back. As the crowd roars angrily, a punch is thrown, and a violent scrum breaks out on the court steps. The policeman bundles Rozalina from the throng, pausing to check that she is unhurt before running back to help his comrades.

Shaken, Rozalina hurries away down the road, wiping her face with a tissue. Shouts and screams still ring in her ears. It starts to spit with rain, and she is relieved when her battered Volkswagen comes into view. As Rozalina unlocks her car door, she notices that her hand is shaking. Safely inside her car, she slumps back against the seat, and closes her eyes.

There is a loud knock on her window.

Rozalina starts violently, looks up to see a young man in a suit standing by her car, his journalist credentials pressed against the glass. She puts a hand over her heart in a sign of shocked relief, and winds the window down. The man gives her an apologetic smile.

'Sorry to scare you,' he says. 'I was stuck at the back of the crowd at the courthouse, and I wanted to try and speak to you before you drove away. My name is Oleg – I'm a reporter from the *Moscow Times*.'

'Rozalina Petrova,' she replies, shaking his hand.

Oleg nods back at the mayhem still raging on the court steps.

'Ugly stuff. Are you OK?'

'I've seen worse,' says Rozalina. 'Tensions always run high in these sorts of cases.'

'I was wondering whether I could ask you a few questions about the trial . . . ?'

Rozalina taps her steering wheel uncertainly. 'Can we do it tomorrow? It's been a long few weeks, and all I feel like doing is going back to my flat and curling up on the sofa.'

Oleg makes a helpless gesture. 'Today, this is a big story. My editor will put an interview with you on the front page. Tomorrow?' The journalist shrugs. 'Maybe a bomb goes off in Chechnya, or the President has an official trip abroad. Maybe my editor doesn't care about you so much then.'

Rozalina isn't interested in seeing her face on the front page of newspapers. However, she knows all too well the struggles her clients face in trying to get justice – the intimidation from their attackers, the occasional apathy of the police. Success stories like Borovsky's conviction need to be heard by as many people as possible.

'OK,' she says, reluctantly. 'But it'll have to be in my flat, and I can't remember the last time I cleaned it.'

Oleg laughs as he climbs in the car. 'Don't worry – you should see my place.'

They drive through Moscow back towards Rozalina's flat, making awkward small talk about the traffic and the weather. The rain picks up in intensity, hammering on to the roof and streaming down the windshield. In the cramped confines of her Volkswagen, Rozalina is suddenly very aware of the stranger's proximity. Up close, there is something naggingly familiar about Oleg's face – but then she presumes he has been reporting from the courtroom throughout the trial. Though the man is unfailingly polite, Rozalina is beginning to regret agreeing to the interview.

It takes them half an hour to navigate back to Rozalina's apartment block. Pleased to escape the car, she gets out, retrieving a bag full of groceries from her boot.

'I bought these last night,' she explains. 'What with everything going on, I completely forgot about them.'

'I'm not surprised,' laughs Oleg again.

Rozalina enters the block and climbs wearily up the stairs to the fourth floor, propping her groceries against her apartment door as she unlocks it. After the ugliness outside the courthouse, and the miserable weather, her flat feels as warm and inviting as a bath.

'Lock the door behind you, will you?' she calls out over her shoulder, placing her groceries carefully down on to the kitchen table. 'Tea?'

'Thanks,' answers Oleg. As Rozalina puts on the kettle, he looks inquisitively around the flat. 'Nice place,' he says.

'You're very polite,' replies Rozalina. She makes two cups of sugary tea and carries them over to the sofa, where Oleg sits inspecting a photograph of Rozalina's nephew on the low table in front of him.

'You must be pleased to see Borovsky behind bars,' he says.

'I'm always pleased to see a murderer behind bars,' she replies, taking a cautious sip of hot tea.

'Naturally,' Oleg says casually, picking up the photograph. 'Though you're aware that not everyone shares your opinion. Some Russians think that Nikolai Borovsky is a hero.'

'A hero?' Rozalina laughs incredulously. 'I don't know that murdering innocent people simply because they're a different nationality counts as an act of heroism. Men like Borovsky are fascist bullies, and they give ordinary

Russians a bad name. Someone has to stand up to them.' She pauses. 'Don't you want to write this down?'

Oleg places the photograph back on the table and shakes his head very slowly. The cosy atmosphere in the flat takes on a colder edge. Rozalina suddenly realizes that something is very, very wrong.

'You're not a journalist,' she says quietly. Not a question.

Oleg smiles dangerously.

As he springs to his feet, Rozalina hurls her tea in his face, but the man doesn't even flinch. Oleg is on her in a second, wrapping a hand over her mouth, staunching her screams.

'Marat!' he shouts.

The door to Rozalina's flat flings open, and a blond teenager with cropped hair strides inside. Her heart sinking, Rozalina remembers she had asked Oleg to lock it.

'Help me with this pig, will you?' he shouts to the boy.

Marat pulls out a hypodermic needle from his pocket and flicks off the cap. Rozalina's eyes widen in terror – frantically she tries to squirm free, but Oleg's grip is as tight and remorseless as a vice. The teenager grins as he approaches.

'Sweet dreams,' he says mockingly.

Rozalina feels a stabbing pain in her thigh, and slowly her fear ebbs away and the world drifts out of focus.

If any of the tenants of Rozalina Petrova's apartment block had been staring out of the windows that afternoon, through the teeming rain they would have seen two men hurrying from the building, one carrying the slumped form of a woman in his arms. Maybe they would have thought it odd; maybe they would have rung the police. But the windows of the nearby flats were all empty, and so there were no witnesses as the woman was dumped in the back of a white van, and the vehicle was hurriedly driven off with a squeal of tyres.

5. War Heroes

As soon as he woke up in the spare room of his uncle's flat, Alexei's mind was flooded by a series of images from the previous day: the barrage of punches overwhelming him in the ring; Lena in the hospital bed, her beautiful face battered; Darius Jordan's dark proposal. His heart heavy, Alexei rolled over and pulled the covers over his head, but his mind was working too frantically to let him fall back to sleep. Reluctantly he dragged himself out of bed.

Alexei pulled on a tatty T-shirt and wandered into the kitchen, where his uncle was stirring a pot of kasha on the stove. Stepan Zhukov was in his sixties, his hair silvery and his imposing frame beginning to sag. As a child, Alexei had been intimidated by his uncle's burly physique and his gruff manner; now he was older, he could appreciate Stepan's dry sense of humour and quiet compassion.

Stepan winced at the sight of his nephew's face. 'I take it the fight didn't go well, then?'

'Not for me.' Slumping down at the table with a sigh, Alexei watched as his uncle doled out two portions of porridge from the saucepan.

'You must have got in late last night,' Stepan said. 'I didn't hear you.'

'Yeah.' Alexei ran a hand through his ruffled hair. 'Uncle, there's something I have to tell you.'

Stepan listened with disbelief to his nephew's story, spluttering into his porridge when he learned what had befallen Lena.

'Dear God!' he exclaimed. 'This is monstrous – what kind of animals would do such a thing? Why didn't you call me?'

'I don't know,' Alexei replied truthfully. 'Everything happened so quickly, I wasn't thinking straight.'

He decided not to tell Stepan about Trojan Industries. In the cold light of day, the idea that he had been asked to become a secret agent seemed ridiculous. His uncle would probably think he was making it up, or that the shock of Lena's assault had somehow affected his mind.

'Have the police said anything?' asked Stepan. 'Are they going to catch these thugs?'

'They haven't spoken to me yet. I'm going back to the hospital today – maybe they'll be there.'

'Do you want me to come with you?'

Alexei shook his head. 'Not today. I need some time alone with her.'

Stepan patted his hand. 'I'll go tomorrow,' he said softly. 'Give her my love.'

After showering and getting dressed, Alexei walked slowly towards the hospital, unsure whether he could face seeing Lena hooked up to all those machines again. In the street, he passed a young couple walking hand-in-hand; the girl giggled as her boyfriend whispered something in her ear. Seeing them gave Alexei a dull pain in the chest.

The nurse behind the hospital reception desk was the

same as the previous evening – she nodded at Alexei as he walked past. Half-expecting to find Darius Jordan waiting for him in Lena's room, instead Alexei was confronted by the sight of Adrine Saroyan sitting at her daughter's bedside, her pale face streaked with tears.

'Hi,' Alexei said uncertainly.

At first Lena's mother didn't reply. Then she sprang to her feet and began beating her fists on his chest.

'Where were you?' she shouted. 'Where were you when they did this?'

Alexei stood dumbly, at a loss for words. What on earth could he say? How could he defend himself? He realized that Adrine had stopped hitting him, and had dissolved into tears on his shoulder.

'I'm sorry,' she sobbed. 'But how could they do this to my daughter, my beautiful Lena?'

'It's OK,' Alexei said softly, awkwardly putting his arms around her. 'It'll be all right. I promise.'

Eventually Adrine's tears subsided, and they sat quietly by Lena's side, watching her chest rise and fall as she breathed. The heart monitor continued its slow, metronomic bleeping.

'What if she doesn't wake up, Alexei?' Lena's mother whispered, at one point.

'She'll wake up. Lena's a fighter – you know that.'

Even though he tried to sound confident, to Alexei his were hollow words. The horrible truth was that he had no idea whether Lena would wake up again. If only she hadn't won that stupid modelling competition! Then they wouldn't have moved to Moscow, and instead of being trapped in this airless hospital room they'd be messing around with their school friends back in Volgograd.

Alexei was keenly aware that Darius Jordan's business card was still sitting in his pocket. The American had given him a day to give Trojan his answer. It would be madness to volunteer to work for him, but what would happen if he said no? What would they do to him? More importantly, what would they do to Lena?

Too many questions. Not enough answers. Alexei said farewell to Adrine and trudged home, feeling completely and utterly lost.

The first thing Alexei noticed as he returned to Stepan's flat was the acrid smell of cigarettes. The sound of voices filtered through from the sitting room. Cautiously, Alexei peered round the door.

His uncle was sat in his favourite chair, leaning forward as he talked animatedly. A slim woman with a dark-brown ponytail was sitting opposite him, a pair of sunglasses pushed up on her head, curls of smoke rising up from her cigarette and out of the open window. Alexei's eyes widened as he recognized her – the last time he had seen this woman, she had been sitting in the front seat of Darius Jordan's people carrier.

'Come in, Alexei, come in,' urged Stepan. 'This is Dr Valerie Singer. She's come from Moscow State University to discuss your future. Isn't that an honour?'

'It's a surprise, all right,' Alexei replied carefully. He gave the woman a meaningful look. 'But I'm not sure there's that much to talk about.'

'Don't be so sure,' said Valerie, surprising Alexei by speaking in flawless Russian. 'At least not until you've heard our offer. All through the spring we run short training courses at MSU – designed to give potential students an idea of university life. They're only two weeks long – hard work, but very rewarding. Our engineering course has had a last-minute dropout, and we were sufficiently impressed by your academic record back in Volgograd to offer you the place.'

'These courses sound very prestigious,' Stepan added excitedly. 'They could really help your chances of enrolling properly in the autumn, Alexei. What do you say?'

Alexei shook his head. 'I think you've got the wrong person,' he said coolly. 'I think you'd better leave.'

'Manners, Alexei!' scolded Stepan. 'Please forgive my nephew,' he said apologetically to Valerie. 'There's been a dreadful incident concerning someone very close to him, and as you can imagine it's affecting him.'

'I'm sorry to hear that,' replied Valerie. She stubbed out her cigarette in the ashtray. 'Your uncle was telling me all about your grandfather, Alexei. I didn't realize he was a war hero.'

'He was given the Medal for the Defence of Stalingrad,' Stepan said proudly. 'Helped keep those bastard Nazis out of the city. Of course, there was a terrible cost – two million people died, Alexei! And not just soldiers, but ordinary people; men, women and children, joining together to beat back Hitler's hordes. Heroes, all of them. I used to pester my father with questions about Stalingrad, but he'd never talk about it. No one who survived did. But I know how proud he was when Alexei's father and I followed him into the army.'

Alexei had heard the story countless times before, but he knew better than to interrupt. Stepan was lost in his father's story, a catch of emotion in his voice as he spoke.

'My mother was born in Leningrad,' said Valerie. 'She lost her father in 1942. She ended up moving all the way to Israel to escape the memories.'

'All those lives lost, and turned upside down, and for what?' Stepan said bitterly. 'After all that our forefathers sacrificed, today we have Nazis walking the streets – Russian streets! Like these . . . *scum* . . . who attacked Alexei's girlfriend. If I was ten years younger myself . . .'

His voice trailed off.

'It's not your battle to fight any more,' Valerie said. She looked pointedly at Alexei. 'It's down to the next generation to continue the struggle.'

Stepan harrumphed. 'Kids these days. How could they understand?'

'It's up to us to make them, Stepan.'

There was a long pause. Alexei glanced at his uncle, his eyes misty with emotion, and then back to Valerie. 'OK,' he said quietly. 'You've made your point. I'll sign up to your course.'

'I thought you'd come round to my way of thinking.' Valerie rose from her chair. 'Lovely to meet you, Stepan,' she said.

'You're leaving already?' Alexei's uncle asked, bewildered.

'Time is against us, and there are a lot of forms to fill

in before Alexei can start. Don't worry – he'll be very comfortable in university accommodation.'

'He's going to stay at MSU?'

'It's a very intensive course, Mr Zhukov,' Valerie said smoothly. 'I'd imagine Alexei's going to be very busy for the foreseeable future.'

Stepan glanced at Alexei. 'What about Lena?'

'I'll make time to see her,' Alexei replied firmly. 'Believe me.'

'Well, if you're both sure . . .' Startled into submission by the pace of events, Stepan waited for Alexei to throw some clothes into a bag and then showed them both to the door.

'Call me when you get the chance,' he instructed his nephew, giving him a quick encouraging smile.

Valerie kissed Stepan warmly on both cheeks, then accompanied Alexei out of the apartment building and into the weak spring sunshine. Alexei was unsurprised to see the people carrier waiting for them outside, the driver from the previous night still behind the wheel. Before they climbed in, Alexei grabbed Valerie's arm.

'If I agree to do this,' he said, 'I want constant updates on Lena. When she wakes up, I want to know about it.'

'That can be arranged.'

'And I don't want to see anyone from Trojan at my uncle's apartment again. This has got nothing to do with him, and I don't want him finding out about it.'

Valerie Singer pushed her sunglasses down over her eyes. 'About time you showed some backbone,' she said, her tone icy. 'Now let's get to work.'

6. Dangerous Company

The people carrier crawled through Moscow, inching its way along motorway lanes banked up with cars. For twenty minutes, none of its inhabitants said a word, until yet another snarl-up made the driver blow out his cheeks with exasperation.

'Bloody traffic!' he exclaimed in an English accent. 'This is even worse than London!'

'Moscow traffic jams: best in Europe,' Valerie replied laconically. 'Why do you think the underground is so good?'

They headed south-east towards the Taganka district, where the traffic finally began to dissolve, and the driver was able to open up the engine. Roaring up a steep hill, the people carrier turned off the main road at the summit, bouncing through a stone archway on to a gravel track. As the track curved round through a small wood, a grand building appeared on the horizon, crowned by an onion-shaped cupola supported by a cluster of narrow bell-towers. A golden cross stood proudly on top of the dome. The people carrier crunched to a halt outside the front porch, and Valerie gestured at Alexei to get out. On closer inspection, the building had fallen into disrepair, its whitewashed walls covered in grime and graffiti, its arched windows boarded up.

'What is this place?' asked Alexei.

'Couple of hundred years ago, it was a monastery,' replied the Englishman. 'Right now, it's Trojan Industries' HQ.'

With a loud bleep, he set the vehicle's alarm, then led Alexei and Valerie through the front porch and inside the building. The monastery was cold and dark, and it took Alexei's eyes several seconds to accustom themselves to the gloom. He was standing in a narrow passageway with a ceiling so low it brushed his head.

'Mind your footing,' the Englishman warned. 'Don't want you injuring yourself before you've even started.'

Alexei followed him along the corridor, careful to avoid the potholes and loose flagstones that lay in wait for unwary footsteps. At the end of the passageway, the Englishman pushed open a heavy wooden door.

Alexei blinked.

The vast hall beyond was in a ruinous state, cluttered with piles of rubble and rotten planks. The religious paintings on the walls had been chipped away until only glimpses of wide-eyed saints' faces remained. Holes gaped in the roof like missing teeth, and as Alexei entered the hall he had to weave a path through a series of buckets laid out on the floor to catch rainwater. Up in the rafters, there came the sound of beating birds' wings, and wind whistled viciously through the gaps in the boarded-up windows.

Despite the musty atmosphere, the contents of the

hall were decidedly twenty-first century. A bank of slim laptops was ranged along a workbench, with a row of young operatives tapping away on the keys. Large flat-screen televisions cut from live news feeds to CCTV footage and satellite images of Moscow. Portable spotlights on stands hummed as they lit up the room. At the centre of it all stood Darius Jordan, stroking his chin thoughtfully as he studied a large electronic map of the Russian capital. At the sight of Alexei, he smiled and strode over to give him a bone-crushing handshake.

'Good to see you, son,' he said, his baritone voice echoing around the hall. 'I hear you've decided to work with us.'

Alexei glanced at Valerie. 'Word gets around fast.'

'We're used to working against the clock,' replied Jordan. 'Let's meet in the briefing room. Ten minutes.'

He turned back to the map, and Alexei realized that their conversation was over. The briefing room turned out to be a dilapidated antechamber leading off from the hall, kitted out with a conference table, a projector and a screen, which was hanging down from the far wall. As he waited alone for Darius Jordan, Alexei nervously poured himself a glass of water. Up until now, a part of him had been convinced that all this was some kind of elaborate hoax, but the scale of the operation in the monastery left him in no doubt: this was for real, all right.

It wasn't long before Jordan returned, carrying a laptop, which he connected up to the projector. Valerie and the Englishman followed him into the room, the driver closing the door behind him. Jordan nodded towards them.

'Alexei, you've already met Valerie Singer, head of Human Resources, and Richard Madison, head of Technical Support. They'll be your main contacts here at Trojan. Valerie is ex-Mossad – Israeli secret service – and Richard worked for the Secret Intelligence Service in Britain, so rest assured you're in safe hands.'

'What about you?' Alexei asked Jordan. 'Where do you come from?'

The American gave him a gleaming smile. 'Let's just say I'm a man of the world.'

'I don't understand,' Alexei said. 'If these guys are such hotshots, why don't they take out this gang? Why do you need me?'

'That's the first sensible thing the boy's said all day,' Valerie said darkly.

Jordan shot her a warning glance. 'You've made your feelings on that point very clear, Miss Singer. But the objective of this mission is to discover the full extent of the Eagles' organization, so we can make sure that every diseased root of the gang is ripped out from the ground. That will not be achieved by simply killing skinheads. And in any case, Trojan is *not* a team of vigilante assassins – no matter how much you'd like it to be on certain occasions.'

Valerie muttered something in Russian under her breath, and lit another cigarette.

'Now,' said Jordan, 'if we can proceed to the matter at hand.' He pressed a key on his laptop, and a photograph of a closed shop-front appeared on the projector screen. Two figure eights had been daubed on to the metal shutters in red paint, separated by a swastika symbol. Jordan sat on the edge of the table and pointed at the screen.

'This is the tag of our main target: the Moscow Eagle 88s.'

Alexei frowned. 'What does the 88 mean?'

'It's a kind of code – corresponds to two letter Hs.'

'Short for Heil Hitler,' Richard Madison chipped in. 'Just in case the swastika isn't enough of a clue.'

'Quite,' said Jordan. 'Now, experts estimate that there are at least fifty neo-Nazi gangs in Russia – but these guys are the toughest, no question. Their main enforcer is the man whose picture I showed you in the newspaper – Nikolai Borovsky. He was convicted of murder this afternoon, but even with him behind bars the Moscow Eagles still pose a very real threat.'

He pressed the key again. The graffiti was replaced by a photograph of a crowd of skinheads pressed menacingly up against a wire fence, their fists clenched and raised in the air as they shouted.

'And here are the 88s in full flow. This was taken during a demonstration at a building site run by Construktko – a construction company owned by a Muscovite tycoon called Boris Lebedev. The Eagles were protesting about the fact that Lebedev hires too many immigrants for their liking, meaning there are fewer jobs for native Russians like themselves. Soon after this photograph, the demonstration descended into a riot – the Eagles pulled down the fence and smashed up the site. Three Construktko workers ended up in hospital. You can see Nikolai Borovsky leading the protests. But he's not the man I want you to focus on.'

Jordan pointed to a figure standing apart from the Eagles, only half in shot. Alexei guessed the man must have been in his mid-forties, lean-faced and smartly dressed. A pair of horn-rimmed spectacles perched on the bridge of his nose, beneath sandy-coloured hair combed into a neat side-parting.

'This charmer is Viktor Orlov,' said Jordan. 'It's a rare public shot of him. Viktor's clever enough never to get his hands dirty, but he's the brains of the outfit – the *de facto* leader. If you're going to succeed in your assignment, and find out the extent of the Eagles' organization, earning Viktor's trust is going to be absolutely crucial.'

'Easier for you to say,' said Alexei. 'How am I supposed to make friends with a bunch of Nazis?'

'With Borovsky out of the picture, the Eagles will be in a state of reorganization. It's the perfect time to introduce yourself. Technical Support will fill you in on the details. We can't be sure yet how long we've got until your mission is initiated, but we'll make use of every available second.'

There was a knock at the door, and a man looked into the room.

'Sorry to interrupt, Mr Jordan, but there's something you need to look at.'

The American turned to Alexei. 'Seems I'm going to have to leave you in Richard's capable hands,' he said. 'Good luck, son.'

He strode out of the room with Valerie, leaving Alexei alone with the Englishman. Madison looked up at the photograph of Viktor Orlov.

'Don't know what you look so worried about,' he said drily. 'Sounds like a piece of piss to me.'

Alexei laughed humourlessly.

'It's not all bad news, you know,' Madison continued. 'With your kickboxing background, if there's any trouble at least you can take care of yourself until the cavalry arrives.'

'You obviously didn't see my last fight,' Alexei said gloomily.

Madison grinned. 'You sound just like our Brazilian agent,' he said. 'He took some convincing at first, too.'

'Oh yeah? And how did things work out for him?'

The Englishman nodded. 'Not bloody bad. He made it out the other side. Busted the nastiest gang in Rio to boot.' He patted Alexei on the back. 'And I've every confidence you'll be just as successful. Trojan only selects the best, Alexei. We don't make mistakes.'

Despite Madison's encouragement, as he stared at the photograph of the skinhead gang, Alexei felt anything but confident.

'I hate to interrupt this touching scene, but . . .'

They turned round to see Valerie Singer standing in the doorway. 'Looks like events have overtaken us,' she said. 'You'd better come and see this.'

Back in the main hall, Darius Jordan was standing in front of a television screen, watching a local news programme. A glamorous blonde woman with a serious expression was addressing the camera.

'Only hours after today's conviction of the neo-Nazi Nikolai Borovsky for murder, this station was sent a videotape claiming to show Rozalina Petrova, a human rights lawyer and key figure behind Borovsky's guilty verdict. Experts have analysed the recording, and confirmed its authenticity.'

The picture changed to grainy, hand-held video footage of a middle-aged woman sitting in a chair in front of a giant Nazi flag, her head slumped forward on to her chest. Three men in balaclavas were standing guard around her. One of them lifted her head to show her face to the camera.

'She doesn't look like she knows what day it is,' said Alexei.

'They've drugged her,' Jordan replied grimly.

The screen cut back to the news studio. 'In the video,' the newsreader continued, 'the men state that the Russian authorities have ten days to free the convicted Borovsky from prison, or Ms Petrova will be executed. So far the Russian Justice Ministry has been unavailable for comment.'

Alexei glanced at Jordan.

'Do you think this is the Eagles?'

'I don't think,' the American replied. 'I *know*.'

He turned to Richard Madison. 'Whatever training programmes you were planning to run through with Alexei, we need to get to operational mode as soon as possible.' Darius Jordan looked back again at the screen, which was displaying a close-up of Rozalina Petrova's woozy face. 'There's no time to waste.'

7. Clock Watching

Forty-two hours. Alexei stared at the large LED timer on the monastery wall as it counted down, willing it to stop. There were only forty-two hours until mission commencement – which Darius Jordan had scheduled for 1100 hours the day after next. It felt like both a lifetime and a heartbeat away.

Alexei was sitting gloomily in a chair while a pretty young make-up artist called Yelena bustled around him. Ordinarily he would have enjoyed chatting to her, but as she carefully shaved the hair from his head he could feel himself trembling.

Yelena turned off the razor and inspected Alexei's skinhead, finally nodding with approval. 'You're starting to look the part,' she said.

'Do you do this a lot?' he asked.

Yelena laughed. 'Not in these conditions. Usually I work on movies. Trojan hired me as an "outside consultant" – whatever that means. They pay me too well to ask any questions.' She smiled. 'Right, time for stage two. You need to take your top off.'

Alexei did as he was told, feeling both cold in the draughty hall and acutely self-conscious. Yelena picked up a metal object shaped like a small pistol, a power cord snaking away from its base. She inspected the tip carefully.

'What's that?' Alexei asked.

'A tattoo gun,' replied the make-up artist. 'I was told to give you a swastika tattoo.'

'What?' yelled Alexei, half-leaping out of his chair.

'It'll be OK,' Yelena said reassuringly. 'We can laser it off afterwards. You'll barely have a mark on you.'

'I don't care!' Alexei shouted. 'No way you're putting that on me!' As Richard Madison hurried over towards him, he yelled 'This is bullshit!' at the Englishman.'

'This is the exact opposite of bullshit,' Madison replied sharply. 'This is exactly what you need. You're a Moscow Eagle now. You need to talk like them, act like them, and you need to bloody look like them too. If we stick some kind of temporary tattoo on you, they'll spot it in seconds, and you'll be done for.'

The Englishman crouched down beside him, and carried on in a softer voice. 'It's all right to be nervous, Alexei. God knows, I've seen agents with a damn sight more field experience than you freak out before a mission. Understand that I wouldn't put you through this if I didn't think it was crucial. I promise you we'll remove the tattoo when your mission's over. Yelena's expertise doesn't end with hairclippers and make-up. You have to trust us, Alexei. Can you do that?'

Alexei turned his head away, then nodded, He closed his eyes as Yelena turned on the tattoo gun, which immediately began buzzing like a hornet. As the needle bit into his chest, Alexei gritted his teeth to stop himself crying out. The tattoo seemed to take forever, every line of ink demanding another insistent scratch of the needle against his skin. In an attempt to block out the pain, Alexei flooded his mind with happy memories of him and Lena back in Volgograd, when no dream had seemed impossible and the future offered only bright possibilities.

Afterwards, as he inspected the black symbol on his pink, raw skin in a mirror, Alexei had to blink back the tears. Yelena touched his arm sympathetically.

'I know it looks like it'll be there forever,' she said quietly. 'But it'll gone before you know it.'

It was all Alexei could do to nod mutely.

After dinner, Darius Jordan ordered Alexei to phone his uncle and reassure him that he was settling in. Stepan bombarded him with so many questions about the university and his fictitious course that Alexei quickly began to falter. In the middle of a stammering lie about his accommodation, Valerie Singer appeared at his shoulder and beckoned at him to pass her the phone. She was soon charming Stepan, and in under a minute she had snapped the phone shut and tossed it back to Alexei.

'You're never that nice to me,' he said.

'Work on your lying,' Valerie replied icily. 'That was just your uncle. Stutter like that in front of the Eagles and you're a dead man.'

That night Alexei snatched three hours of sleep dozing in a cot in the corner of the hall. He was awoken by Darius Jordan dropping a file on to his bed.

'What's this?' Alexei asked sleepily.

'Your backstory,' the American replied. 'The Eagles

are going to want to know about you before they trust you, so I'd advise you learn this thoroughly. You can keep your first name – it's common enough, and the fewer lies you have to tell the better. Breakfast in five minutes.'

Looking up at the LED clock with a heavy heart, Alexei saw that there were only twenty-eight hours left. Rozalina Petrova's kidnap had shortened what little time there had been for his training – it felt like every time he turned around, Alexei was being fed new information by one Trojan operative or another. He was dizzy with the speed at which people moved, their clipped efficiency betraying their military backgrounds. Only Richard Madison maintained an easy-going facade. Later that morning, Alexei was summoned to one of the monastery's antechambers to find the Englishman reading a history book on Josef Stalin, his feet propped up on the table by a laptop.

'Have a seat,' he said breezily, snapping the book shut. 'I was just doing some background reading.'

'You interested in communism?' Alexei asked.

'A little,' Madison replied. 'How about you? Ever find yourself hankering for the good old days of the Cold War?'

Alexei shrugged. 'Before my time,' he said. 'Politicians are all the same, anyway. Whoever's in charge, they only care about lining their own pockets.'

'You may have a point there,' Madison said wryly. 'I can't help but wonder whether you'd have such a problem with neo-Nazi gangs in the old days, though. When your country was still the Soviet Union, internal travel restrictions meant that immigration could be kept under tighter control. These days, it's a lot easier for a poor man in the former Soviet republics – in Chechnya, say, or Tajikistan, or Azerbaijan – to come to Moscow in hope of getting a better-paid job in the big city. Problem is, that spawns the kind of discontent that the Moscow Eagles thrive on.' He blew out his cheeks. 'You know, Alexei, we've studied gangs all around the world. Ninety per cent of the time, gangs get new members for the same reasons: people want respect or protection, or think it's the only way they can make money. In some of the hellholes I've visited, you can almost understand them. The 88s aren't like that. The only thing they've got in common, the only glue that binds them, is racial hatred. Every foreigner is a "black" to them, every "black" is inferior. Street riots and punishment beatings are their stock in trade. In conclusion: the quicker we can shut them down the better.'

Calling up a virtual map of Moscow on a laptop, the Englishman zoomed in on a building off Komsomolskaya Square – a rundown area in the north-east of the capital.

'Now, this is the dragon's lair,' Madison explained. 'It's a gym run by the Eagles. We'll take you there tomorrow morning. Remember: first impressions count for a lot around these guys. It's not just about skinheads and tattoos; it's about attitude. Don't think – don't doubt. I know we're asking a lot of you. But if you complete this mission, it'll be worth it. Never forget that.'

Alexei nodded. 'I won't.'

'Good lad,' said Madison. 'I'm sorry we don't have

more time to get you ready. This might help make up for it, though.'

The Englishman pressed a tiny metallic disc several millimetres in diameter into Alexei's palm. Alexei turned it over in his hand.

'What's this?'

'This, my friend, is the height of miniaturized technology. It's a bug. Not only will it record everything it picks up with superb sound quality, but you can even phone it and listen in live over your mobile. It's quad band, so you could call from the Amazon jungle and it'd sound like you're in the same room. If you can find somewhere to plant it around the Eagles, we'll hear exactly what they're saying in private. This is a bloody high-tech piece of kit – so for God's sake don't drop it down the toilet, or something stupid like that.'

For the first time in what felt like an age, Alexei smiled. 'I'll do my best,' he said, slipping the disc into the pocket of his wallet.

That evening, he insisted on being taken back to the hospital. In the stillness of Lena's room, Alexei felt the doubts temporarily close in over his head, but one glance at the marks of abuse on her face stiffened his resolve. Deep down, he knew that she would have said he was doing the right thing. Knowing Lena, she would probably have wanted to do it herself. Alexei leaned forward and kissed her softly on the forehead.

'I'll be back soon,' he whispered. 'I promise.'

He was driven back to the monastery, which continued to hum with activity through the night. Unable to sleep,

Alexei read his backstory over and over again, his eyelids finally falling shut as the sky was lightening, and the LED timer had clicked down to six hours.

A backstreet off Komsomolskaya Square: zero hours until mission commencement. In the back seat of an unmarked Lada, Alexei felt his gut turn another somersault. He had already been sick twice that morning – and even though his stomach was empty, he wanted to throw up again. Accompanied by Valerie and Madison, he had been watching the gym across the street for nearly an hour. In that time, ten Eagles had entered the building.

Madison checked his watch, then looked back from the driver's seat.

'Ready?'

Alexei took a deep breath. 'Guess so.' He looked over at Valerie. 'Any last-minute words of advice?'

The Israeli woman gazed levelly at Alexei, then answered in Russian: 'If you get a chance to kill any of them, don't hesitate. I'll cover you with Trojan.'

Richard Madison gave Valerie a questioning glance, but she didn't elaborate, coolly selecting another cigarette from a battered packet.

It was time. Alexei picked up his kitbag and got out of the Lada. As he crossed the street, he saw a teenage girl leave the gym and sit down on the pavement by the door. She was dressed in a short purple dress and ripped black tights, and her hair was streaked with blonde highlights. Pulling out a mobile phone, she began texting, a look of sour boredom on her face.

'You going inside?' she called out as Alexei walked past her.

He stopped. 'Maybe. Why?'

'Maybe you're not welcome.'

Alexei looked pointedly up at the sign above the door, and then back at his kitbag. 'It is a gym, right? It's got weights, punchbags, that kind of thing?'

'*Private* gym,' the girl corrected him tartly. 'They don't like strangers.'

Alexei gave the girl what he hoped was a winning smile. 'Then how about you put in a word for me?'

She looked away, uninterested.

With a shrug, Alexei walked through the door and into the gloomy interior. The Moscow Eagles' gym was dominated by a raised ring in the centre of the room, surrounded by square blue training mats. Punchbags hung down from the ceiling like slabs of beef in a meat locker. Old posters advertising boxing matches were peeling away from the walls, and dumbbells and weights were scattered across the floor.

It looked like every other gym Alexei had spent time training in – with one major difference. No one was actually working out. Instead, a group of burly men had congregated around the benches at one side of the room, talking in low guttural tones. There was an edge to the atmosphere in this room that went beyond concentrated physical training: a suppressed air of violence thicker than the smell of body odour. The men stared at Alexei as he entered, their conversations ending abruptly.

Alexei was almost tempted to turn around and walk

straight out again, but then the thought of Lena came into his head. It was two of these bastards who had attacked her – they could be watching him right now. There was no way he was going to back down. Instead Alexei walked over to the punchbag at the far end of the gym, trying to look unconcerned by the scrutiny. Slowly, deliberately, he dropped his kitbag to the floor and took off his T-shirt, displaying the swastika on his chest. He began working the punchbag, quickly losing himself in familiar combinations of lefts and rights.

As he built up a sweat, Alexei became aware of a teenager breaking away from the knot of men to approach him. A baseball cap was pressed down on his head, half-obscuring his face, and his black-and-white checked shirt was buttoned up to the neck. The teenager stood and watched him train, his arms crossed.

'Nice work,' he said eventually. 'You know what you're doing.'

Alexei ignored him, concentrating on throwing rights into the punchbag.

'Mind if I ask you a question?' the boy continued.

'Knock yourself out,' Alexei replied. 'You're in the right place.'

'Are you crazy or retarded?'

Alexei stopped hitting the bag, a puzzled expression on his face. 'Excuse me?'

'It's just, you've walked into this gym like you own it, and this is the *worst* place to show that kind of disrespect. I reckon you've got about two minutes before you get the shit beaten out of you. My friend reckons you're crazy, but you look pretty sane to me, so I figure you're just retarded. So which one is it?'

Before Alexei could reply, there was a sudden explosion of noise behind them; he turned round to see a muscular man in a sleeveless sweatshirt bursting into the gym, his bald head gleaming in the light. Even from this distance, Alexei saw that the newcomer was built like an ox. The man snarled something back towards the doorway and then stalked across the gym.

'Hey, Medved!' the teenager in the baseball cap called out. 'What's going on?'

The giant skinhead barged past him, nearly knocking the teenager to the ground. Before Alexei could react, Medved strode up and punched him squarely in the face.

8. Hate Figure

Alexei crumpled to the training mat to howls of laughter from the Moscow Eagles. The teenager moved hastily out of the way as the muscular skinhead roared like a bear, and swung a boot at Alexei. The blow caught him flush in the gut; groaning, he clutched at his midriff.

'I'm going to kill you, you little shit!' Medved bellowed.

Through watering eyes, Alexei saw the skinhead raise his boot to stamp down on him – instinctively, he shifted his body position and swept Medved's standing leg from under him. As the skinhead toppled to the ground, Alexei rolled away and struggled to his feet. Immediately the Eagles stopped laughing and ran over to back up Medved. Forcing himself upright, Alexei clenched his fists and prepared himself for the onslaught.

'What the hell's going on here?'

Everyone stopped. Two older men were standing by the entrance to the gym: the speaker was a small, wiry man in combat trousers, a heavy gold necklace hanging over his green T-shirt.

The second was Viktor Orlov.

Even though Alexei had only caught a glimpse of him at the back of a blurry photograph, there was no mistaking the lean, intelligent face and horn-rimmed glasses. Unlike the rest of the Eagles, a burly army clad in jeans and white T-shirts, Viktor was dressed in a suave black suit and long overcoat, his short hair trained into a neat side-parting. He walked calmly into the centre of the ring of men, his companion following a pace behind. The gym was so quiet that the only sound Alexei could hear was his own ragged breaths.

'Pavel asked you a question,' Viktor said quietly. 'I'd appreciate an answer.'

'This bastard tried to hit on my girl!' Medved blustered, pointing an accusatory finger at Alexei.

'What girl?' panted Alexei incredulously, his hands on his knees. 'I don't know what the hell he's talking about!'

Viktor tapped his cheek thoughtfully. 'It seems we have one man's word against another. Only one person can help us resolve this. Pavel?'

The wiry man turned round and called out: 'Svetlana! Get your ass in here!'

There was a few seconds' pause, and then the girl Alexei had seen sitting outside the gym walked sulkily towards them.

'Her?' he said. 'I didn't –'

'No one asked you to speak,' snapped Viktor.

Alexei fell silent. He might have been spared for the moment, but the danger was far from over. If things went wrong here he was outnumbered twelve to one. It looked as though the only way out of the gym was through the front door, and there were at least three burly skinheads standing in his way. He didn't fancy his chances of fighting his way out.

With a cajoling smile, Viktor beckoned Svetlana towards him. She reluctantly allowed the leader of the 88s to pat her on the cheek.

'You need to help us sort this little problem out,' he said. 'Tell Viktor the truth – did this boy come on to you? Don't lie to me now.'

Svetlana looked at Alexei for what felt like an eternity, then shrugged and looked away.

'You see?' said Alexei. 'I didn't do a thing!'

'Shut your mouth!' Medved growled. 'No one talks to my girl – especially not runts like you.'

'Go outside and calm down,' rapped Pavel. 'We'll take it from here.'

Shooting a final murderous glance at Alexei, Medved wrapped a protective arm around Svetlana's shoulder and they walked out of the gym. Viktor waited for the skinhead to leave, then turned back to Alexei.

'Right,' he said sharply. 'Who are you, and what are you doing here?'

'My name's Alexei. I came here because I wanted to train and I wanted to fight. Then that crazy guy came out of nowhere and tried to beat the shit out of me. I didn't mean to cause any disrespect. I thought I'd be welcome here. I *thought* this gym would have my kind of people in it.'

'Really?' said Viktor, raising an eyebrow. 'And what sort of people would they be?'

Alexei puffed out his chest, displaying his swastika.

'White people,' he said. His words hung in the stale air.

'I see,' Viktor said slowly. 'Well, you may think you know us, Alexei, but we don't know you. And maybe this isn't the best time for us to be inviting strangers into our house.'

'Whatever you say,' Alexei replied. 'All I know is us whites have got to stick together.'

Viktor glanced over at the blond teenager in the baseball cap.

'You know this guy, Marat?'

Marat shook his head. 'He's only been here ten minutes. Looks like he can take care of himself, though. And you know what Medved's like around Svetlana. He thinks anyone who looks at her is trying to bone her.'

The teenager wilted under a caustic look from Viktor. Alexei could taste the tension in the air as the Eagles waited for their leader to pass judgement. After what seemed like an age, Viktor smiled thinly.

'OK, Alexei. We'll say this is all a big . . . *misunderstanding*.' The gang laughed. 'Let's go and have a talk over a drink. There is much to discuss. And someone go tell Medved to leave Alexei alone. For now,' Viktor added, his eyes glinting.

Alexei followed the Eagles out of the gym, tenderly checking his nose. It had been broken before in the ring; mercifully, given how hard Medved had hit him, that didn't seem to be the case now. His stomach was still aching, but he was just relieved to be alive. Ahead of him, the gang swaggered through the deserted streets like a pack of hyenas, their laughter echoing off the scarred factories that lined the route. A train rattled along the tracks past them, heading to one of the stations at Komsomolskaya Square.

A cry went up from the Eagles: someone had spotted an African man on the other side of the street. Seeing the gang of skinheads, the immigrant scurried away to a chorus of jeers and insults. One of the Eagles picked up an empty bottle out of the gutter and hurled it after him. As the glass shattered against the wall, Viktor stopped the man from giving chase.

'Another time,' he said. 'Now we eat and drink.'

They cut down a narrow alleyway and descended a flight of stone steps into an underground bar. The only person inside was a bored-looking bartender, who nodded at Viktor as they entered. Looking around the dirty, gloomy interior, Alexei doubted that the place was going to get any busier.

As the gang settled around a long wooden table, Viktor ordered a bottle of vodka from the barman, and with great ceremony poured out a glass of the colourless liquid for each of his men.

'Drinks!' Viktor called out. He turned to Alexei. 'And why don't we let our new friend propose a suitable toast?'

Alexei coughed nervously. The rest of the table turned expectantly as he rose to his feet, his mind working furiously. Then, it came to him. He raised his glass.

'To Nikolai Borovsky!' he shouted. 'The hero of White Russia!'

The Moscow Eagles roared with approval. Alexei

threw back his head and drained his vodka, feeling the liquid chart a burning course down his throat. As he slammed his glass back on to the table, one of the men barked '*Sieg Heil!*' and made a Nazi salute.

Someone patted Alexei on the back; another put a beer in front of him. He had passed the first test. As the Eagles began rowdily talking with one another, Alexei cautiously sized up the different gang members. He couldn't help wondering which of them had been responsible for the attack on Lena, had callously punched and kicked her into unconsciousness. One thing was certain: no matter what happened with Trojan or Rozalina Petrova, one way or another Alexei would have his private revenge.

The anger was good for him – helped subdue his nerves. He didn't even blink when Medved reappeared. The burly man ignored him, buying a jug of beer before sitting pointedly at the other end of the table. Thankfully Svetlana was nowhere in sight.

Alexei drank quickly, wanting to fit in with the rest of the gang. It was getting harder to stay alert. He noticed that Viktor had barely touched his vodka – the leader of the Eagles seemed content to watch his men get drunk. After a couple of hours Alexei staggered to the bathroom and splashed water on his face in an effort to sober up. He returned to the table to find Viktor refilling his glass.

'So, my young troublemaker,' the man said expansively. 'What brought you to our gym this morning?'

'I told you: I wanted to train.'

'But why a gym run by the Moscow Eagles?'

Trying to clear his head, Alexei thought back to the file Darius Jordan had made him memorize. 'My father died during the war in Chechnya,' he lied.

'I'm sorry to hear that.'

'The filthy bastards got him with a car bomb. That was the only way they could have touched him. He was a hero. Like Borovsky is a hero. Men like him should get medals, not prison sentences.'

Viktor nodded in agreement. 'Wise words for a young man, Alexei. I am sorry to hear about your father – I wish it were an isolated case, but . . .' He pointed at the wiry man in camouflage trousers. 'You see Pavel, there? My right-hand man, my lieutenant. He too fought in Chechnya; lost many good men, many brothers-in-arms. Pavel survives, only to return to Moscow and there is *nothing*. No work, no respect. And yet he sees all these blacks, these half-humans with jobs and money. That is why men like Pavel and you come to us. The Moscow Eagles understand: we are the only family left for White Russians.'

'A family I want to be a part of,' Alexei interjected. 'Borovsky is gone – but maybe one day you'll let me take his place.'

As the leader of the 88s inspected his face thoughtfully, Alexei prayed he had sounded convincing.

'Judging by the bruises on your face, Medved hasn't been the only person punching you recently.'

Alexei shrugged. 'I got into a fight with a couple of bastards from Dagestan. If it had been one-on-one I would have kicked their asses.'

'The foreigners are not stupid. They know that in a *fair* fight with a white they could not hope to win. Which is why we have to play them at their own game.'

'How do we do that?'

Viktor settled back into his chair with a serpentine smile. 'Hang around, and you might well find out,' he said.

9. Street Fighter

They spent all afternoon underground – the cramped bar reverberating with caustic jokes and rough laughter. Drinks were clashed together in toast after toast, sending waves of beer ebbing across the table. In keeping with the Russian superstition, empty bottles were left off the table, forming a small glass platoon on the floor. No one else came down to the bar, and when Alexei helped Marat bring back a round of beers, he noticed that the bartender had the numbers 88 tattooed on his bicep. Just like the gym, this place was clearly for Eagles only.

Eventually Pavel banged on the table for silence. As the conversations broke off and the laughter died, Viktor rose to his feet. He sombrely surveyed the Eagles for several seconds before speaking.

'My friends,' he said finally, opening his arms. 'My white brothers. These have been dark times for us. This week, we have lost a great man, one of our bravest and most steadfast soldiers. Yet again the authorities – overrun by dirty foreigners; infiltrated by sly, deceitful Jews – have betrayed the true Russian heroes, the whites whose struggles and sacrifices provided the foundations for this great nation.'

A murmur of assent rumbled around the table. Even

though Alexei disagreed with Viktor's every word, he couldn't deny that there was something powerful about the way he spoke. The entire bar was hushed in rapt attention.

'Maybe the foreigners think that, with Nikolai in prison, they have won. Maybe the foreigners think that they no longer have to worry about the Moscow Eagles.' Viktor was greeted with loud howls of disapproval. With a smile, he gestured for quiet.

'We need to send them a message that we are going nowhere. A message that will be unmistakable in its tone and its intent. We will send that message with our fists and our feet, and the weapons in our hands.' His voice began to rise in volume. 'And they had better listen! The Chechens, the Armenians, the Tajiks, the Africans and the Jews! None of them will be spared the righteous wrath of the Moscow Eagles! All will feel the might of the White Russian hammer upon them!'

The Eagles rose to their feet, cheering and banging their glasses on the table. Amid the uproar, Viktor leaned over and whispered in Alexei's ear: 'You want to join us, you take part tomorrow. No one can join the Eagles until they have spilt blood.'

Even as he tried to look enthusiastic, Alexei's heart sank.

It was dark by the time Alexei climbed the stairs out of the bar. He took a couple of deep breaths, relishing the cold, crisp air in his lungs. The sound of a chair breaking followed him up the steps: the Eagles were only just starting to party. Alexei had stayed for as long as he could stomach it, until his head was spinning and his words were coming out slurred. In order to leave, he claimed that his girlfriend was nagging him to come home – a statement that caused the rest of the gang no end of amusement. Only Medved continue to glower at him. The skinhead had moodily drained jug after jug of beer, to seemingly no effect.

Alexei got on to the metro at Komsomolskaya Square and headed back towards Taganka. Dozing off in his seat, he nearly missed his stop, only just slipping out through the doors before they shut. He walked back through empty streets and scaled the hill towards the monastery.

The building was dark, the people carrier no longer parked by the entrance, and Alexei was momentarily worried that Trojan Industries had melted away. Hurrying inside, he was relieved to see the electronic equipment pulsing in the glare of the spotlights. Two operatives talked softly to one another as they studied CCTV footage. As Alexei entered the main hall, Richard Madison put down the newspaper he was reading and hurried over to greet him. At the sight of Alexei's dishevelled appearance, the Englishman raised an amused eyebrow.

'Seems some of us have been having more fun than others. You smell like a bloody brewery, son.'

Alexei slumped wearily into a chair. 'Viktor took us to a bar. I tried to stay sober, but they kept topping my drink up.'

'Yeah, that's what they all say. I'll go put some coffee on.'

Madison bustled away, passing Darius Jordan as he appeared out of one of the antechambers. The American instantly noted the marks on Alexei's face. 'Looks like you've already seen some action. What happened?'

Alexei wearily rubbed his eyes. 'I had an argument with one of the Eagles. He won.'

'So the first meeting didn't go well, then?'

'They're pretty tough customers, and they sure as hell don't like strangers. This guy Medved hates my guts, but for now he can't do anything about it because Viktor won't let him.'

'You met Orlov? Did you make a better impression on him?'

'It's hard to tell. He's different from the rest of them – he's smart. He acted all friendly, but I could tell he was checking me out.'

'Don't be fooled by his appearance. Orlov's just as dangerous as the rest of them, if not more so.'

'You don't have to tell me that. He's organizing some kind of raid tomorrow. If I want to join the Eagles, I have to take part in it. I don't know how I'm going to get out of it. Maybe I can say that I'm too hungover or something like that. I mean, obviously I can't go on it . . .'

He trailed off. Jordan said nothing.

'You're not saying I should do it?' Alexei said incredulously.

The American gave him a meaningful look.

'You've got to be kidding me!' Alexei shouted. 'I'm not going to help these guys beat up some poor bastard just because he's foreign!'

For a few seconds Jordan did nothing. Then he nodded. 'I understand completely.' Clapping his hands together, he called out in an echoing voice: 'All right, people! Stop what you're doing and pack it up! We're done here!'

'Hey!' cried Alexei, grabbing the American's arm. 'What are you doing?'

Jordan shrugged. 'If you don't show the Eagles that you're willing to fight with them, they'll never trust you. This has all been a waste of time.' He continued in a low, hard voice. 'You seem to be under the impression that this is some kind of school lesson that you can ask to be excused from. But this is real life, Alexei, and this is your mission. This raid tomorrow will go ahead whether you're there or not. If you don't go, maybe you'll feel better about yourself, but Lena will still be in that hospital and the Eagles will still be out on the streets, free to do it again and again and again.'

Alexei was stung by the sharpness of Jordan's voice. 'It's easy for you to say,' he said bitterly. 'You're not the one who has to attack people. You're not the one who has to get his hands dirty. You don't have to do anything.'

'You think I like that? You think it's easy to ask young people like you to put themselves in danger? Don't forget I *know* what this is like. I've seen things you couldn't begin to imagine, and I've done things you wouldn't want to. If there was any way I could infiltrate the Eagles I would, but I can't. This is the only way we can stop them – no one else is going to do it for us.'

'That still doesn't make this right.'

'You chose to join Trojan, Alexei,' the American replied calmly. 'We didn't force you. So what's it going to be, son: are you in or out?'

Alexei bit his lip, then nodded.

'Good. Before you go to sleep, one of our operatives will interview you. Give them all the information you can.'

Jordan strode out of the hall. Without looking back, he called out over his shoulder: 'You did well today. Keep it up.'

Alexei's head was spinning. All he wanted to do was go to bed, but first he had to spend two hours giving detailed descriptions of the members of the Moscow Eagles. Exhausted and still drunk, when he finally crawled into his cot he instantly fell into a deep, dreamless sleep.

The next morning, the Eagles' gym was taut with anticipation. The skinheads spoke in low, terse sentences as they adjusted their rings and belt buckles, knife blades and screwdriver points glinting in the grimy half-light. Svetlana scurried around them, capturing the preparations on a digital camcorder. The girl's expression of sulky disdain had vanished – she kissed Medved excitedly on the face and neck, looking tiny in his tree-trunk arms.

By contrast, Alexei felt dreadful. His mouth was dry and his head was aching, his hangover only intensified by the dawning realization of what he had agreed to do. He wandered over to Marat, who was working one of the punchbags, the dragon tattoo on his neck seeming to lunge in time with his jabs. At the sight of Alexei's pallid face, the blond teenager smiled.

'I was nervous the first time too,' he said airily. 'You ever hear about the Construktko riot – the one at that guy Lebedev's place?'

Alexei nodded.

'I threw up in the van on the way there. Medved nearly killed me. But once we got stuck in' – Marat punched into the bag for emphasis – 'I was OK. I was better than OK. I loved every second of it.'

Before Alexei could reply, Pavel clapped his hands together and led the Eagles out of the gym. Viktor was nowhere to be seen. As they marched through the streets, Alexei felt overwhelmed by a wave of fear and adrenaline. No laughter broke the grim silence.

They didn't have far to walk: rounding a street corner, Alexei's heart sank at the sight of a group of Uzbek youths milling outside a cafe, laughing and joking with one another as they smoked and drank coffee. Pavel turned and faced the rest of the Eagles, his fist clenched.

'Ready?' he asked.

'For Mother Russia!' bellowed Medved.

The gang let out a primeval roar as they crashed into the Uzbeks, weapons brandished and fists flying. Holding back at the rear of the charge, Alexei froze. This was nothing like fighting in the ring – the Eagles descended upon their victims like a pack of wild dogs, breaking noses on knuckledusters and cracking bones with hammers, bars and chains. A man appeared out of the melee before Alexei, and swung a wild punch in his direction. Alexei ducked out of the way, instinctively responding with a left hook that knocked the man off his feet.

Stunned by the ferocity of the ambush, the Uzbeks scattered like antelope. One or two lay prone in the road, helpless as the Eagles pummelled them with kicks and punches. The air rang with shouts of rage and alarm. Caught up in the confusion, Alexei was nearly knocked over by an Uzbek sprinting past him.

'Get that bastard!' Pavel barked at him.

Alexei turned and gave chase, his heart pounding in his chest. The Uzbek darted left, down a narrow alleyway that ran alongside a restaurant. The path was littered with rubbish; hurdling a pile of wooden crates, Alexei nearly stumbled to the ground. Ahead of him, the Uzbek slipped on a piece of rotten food, and went sprawling into a pile of rubbish bags. Closing in on his target, Alexei saw that the boy was the same age as him, perhaps even younger. Blood trickled from a cut on his forehead down into his eyes. As Alexei stood over him, the Uzbek shielded his head with his hands.

'Get out of here!' hissed Alexei.

The youth stared at him, dumbfounded.

'Are you deaf?' Alexei shouted. 'Get out of here or I'll beat the shit out of you!'

He raised his fist threateningly. The bewildered Uzbek scrambled to his feet and staggered away down the alleyway. When he had disappeared from sight, Alexei let out a deep sigh of relief. If he could convince the Eagles he had been in a proper fight, perhaps they would let him into the gang after all.

Alexei was weighing up his next move when he heard a siren wail, and a police car screeched to a halt at the head of the alleyway.

10. Running Scared

'Hey, you!'

Alexei froze as an officer in a thick leather jacket and fur hat climbed purposefully out of the driver's seat. This was the last thing he needed. If the police thought he was a member of the Moscow Eagles and arrested him Alexei could be in serious trouble. But then Darius Jordan had been clear that if the authorities found out the truth his mission was over. Worse, Alexei had a nasty feeling that he would be left completely on his own – and without Trojan to back him up, who would believe his story?

'Don't move!' warned the policeman.

But Alexei was already running.

He pounded down the alleyway, tipping over crates of mouldy vegetables behind him as he went. The sound of running footsteps pursued him as he reached the wire fence at the end of the passage. Alexei scrambled up the mesh, reached over to the other side and flipped his body over the top feet-first. He dropped down to the ground on the other side, landing heavily on a patch of wasteland. Without pausing, he sprang upright and dashed away through the straggly grass. Alexei didn't dare to look behind him – he didn't need to. He could hear the policeman cursing as he tackled the wire fence. Alexei prayed fervently that he wouldn't pull out his gun and start firing.

He zigzagged across the uneven ground, heading for the shelter of a line of birches at the edge of the wasteland. Alexei exploded through the trees, only to hurriedly skid to a halt on the other side. Just in time. He was teetering on the edge of a steep embankment, overlooking a busy highway that sloped down towards a tunnel. Cars were weaving in and out of the lanes at high speed.

Glancing back through the trees, Alexei saw that the policeman was catching him up, the man's cheeks reddening with exertion. There was nowhere else to go: Alexei grabbed hold of the embankment's edge and lowered himself over the side, his legs scraping against the concrete wall. When he had dangled down as far as he could, he let go, landing in a heap by the side of the highway.

As he picked himself up, Alexei was overwhelmed by petrol fumes and roaring engines. There was no room to run either left or right, and the policeman had reached the edge of the embankment above Alexei's head. The only way out was across six lanes of busy traffic.

'Stop or I'll shoot!' the policeman shouted.

Alexei took a deep breath, and stepped out into the traffic.

He danced across the first lane, feeling a whoosh of air as a car hurtled behind his back. Waiting for a gap in the second lane, Alexei's eyes met those of the female driver, and for a split second the world came to a halt as she stared at him open-mouthed. Then a horn blared at him, her car passed by, and Alexei was on the move again. As he hared across the third lane, he heard someone slamming on the brakes – Alexei didn't bother looking to see who.

At the central reservation, he hurdled over the barrier and rushed out into the second bank of traffic before he could change his mind. The air was choked with a furious chorus of horns. Alexei jockeyed back and forth, only just managing to scramble out of the way of a Mercedes as it changed lanes. He dashed into the final lane – straight into the path of a blue van.

No time to get out of the way. Alexei threw up his hands, his ears filled with loud screeching. He tensed, waiting for the end.

One second passed, then another. Cautiously opening his eyes, Alexei saw that the van's bumper had halted inches from his knees. The smell of burnt tyre rubber singed his nostrils. Placing his hands against the vehicle for support, Alexei walked shakily off the tarmac and up the gentle slope on that side of the highway. The driver in the blue van rolled down his window.

'You bloody idiot!' he bellowed after him. 'Have you got a death wish, you crazy little shit?'

Dazed, Alexei held up an apologetic hand and hurried away. On the other side of the highway, the policeman remained marooned on top of the embankment, his angry shouts drowned out by the traffic.

Alexei took the long way back to the gym, following a nervy, tortuous route through Moscow's backstreets.

Unable to stop his hands trembling, he jammed them into the pockets of his sweatshirt, and pulled the hood over his head. Every time he heard a siren wailing in the distance, he flinched.

As he neared Komsomolskaya Square, Alexei began to calm down, his mind thinking clearly once more. He may have been able to spare the Uzbek, but he still had to look like he had been in a fight. Ducking into a doorway, Alexei gritted his teeth and punched the wall. Pain flared across his knuckles – trying to block it out, he punched the wall again. Suddenly, he felt all the anger and frustration that had been building up within him – the attack on Lena, Trojan's harsh and mysterious dealings; the vileness of the Moscow Eagles – explode to the surface. He wasn't sure how many more times he hit the wall before he finally stopped. Alexei inspected his right fist, breathing heavily. His knuckles were now a purple mass of bruising, blood running down his hands. Good enough.

He was about to cross the street when a police car pulled up outside the gym's entrance. Alexei gasped, and ducked down behind a parked Fiat. As he looked on, a police officer appeared and opened the rear passenger door. Medved hauled himself out. Had he been arrested? What was he doing back here? To Alexei's amazement, the policeman barked with laughter and patted Medved on the back. The skinhead shook his hand warmly and then disappeared inside the gym.

Alexei waited until the police car had driven off before following Medved inside. The pre-fight tension had been replaced by a party atmosphere: the Eagles laughed and joked with one another as they smoked and drank beer. None of them appeared to have sustained any serious injuries. Viktor had reappeared, and was walking around slapping his men on the back. To loud cheers, Medved shook up a bottle of beer and opened it over the rest of the gang like a victorious Formula 1 driver.

'Alexei!' called out Marat, a broad grin on his face. 'Where've you been? You get lost or something?'

'I wish,' Alexei replied. 'Had a run-in with the police – it took me a while to shake them off.' He glanced at Medved. 'Guess I should have just got a lift back like you.'

The giant skinhead shrugged. 'Policemen are just like other Russians. They don't like to see the immigrants dirtying our streets either. They can't say it in public, but they can show their support in other ways. And it's not just policemen, either –'

'I think that's enough,' said Viktor, interrupting him. The leader of the Eagles said it quietly, but Medved immediately fell silent. Viktor fixed his icy blue gaze on Alexei. 'How did you get separated from the rest of the gang?'

'One of the Uzbeks shit himself and ran away down an alleyway,' explained Alexei. 'I went after him.'

'And did you catch him?'

Alexei gingerly displayed his swollen knuckles, earning a nod of approval from Viktor.

'Did he put up much of a fight?' asked Marat eagerly.

'Not for long,' Alexei replied.

'This is good work,' said Pavel, patting Alexei's cheek. 'These vermin have got to learn that they can't just run away. We will follow them down whichever rat hole they flee.' He turned to the rest of the gang, grabbing Alexei's bloodied hand and raising it into the air. 'Let everyone take note: *This* is the fist of a warrior! *This* is the fist of a White Russian! *This* is the fist of a Moscow Eagle!'

The Eagles roared as one. Alexei was submerged beneath a scrum of skinheads, roughly patting him on the head and punching him in the arm. For once, Alexei didn't have to fake his look of relief. He was in.

'It's such a shame . . .' a voice sighed.

The gang stopped and turned to look at Svetlana, who was sitting on a weights bench, curling a lock of hair around her finger like a little girl.

Alexei frowned. 'What's a shame?'

'It's just that your story sounded so exciting,' Svetlana said breathily. 'First you beat up this big bad Uzbek, then you shake off the police. I'd love to include it in my film, but I didn't see it happen. In fact, no one saw it happen.' She grinned maliciously. 'How very . . . *convenient*.'

'Enough, Svetlana!' growled Medved. 'Viktor's said the boy's OK.'

'Who's saying he isn't?' Svetlana replied, her eyes wide with mock innocence. At that moment, Alexei could have quite happily throttled her.

'You're such a shit stirrer,' said Marat. 'Why don't you keep your gob shut?'

Svetlana gave Medved an indignant look. 'Are you going to let him talk to me like that?'

For the first time since Alexei had met him, the burly skinhead seemed unsure of what to do. As Medved faltered, Svetlana snatched up her bag with a shriek of annoyance, and stormed out of the gym.

'You're in trouble there, Medved,' grinned Marat. 'Hope you weren't planning on having sex tonight.'

'You'd better hope he wasn't,' cut in Pavel, 'or it'll be your bedroom door he'll be knocking on to make up for it.'

He slapped Marat on the back with a guttural laugh. Even as the rest of the gang joined in, Alexei felt the hairs on the back of his neck prickle. Out of the corner of his eye, he saw that Viktor was studying him intently, no trace of a smile on his face.

11. Surprise Package

Alexei stood over the Uzbek boy, who was slumped helplessly beneath him on the pile of rubbish bags. The boy looked up at him with pleading eyes.

'I didn't do anything!' he whispered. 'Please . . . !'

Alexei reached down and grabbed the boy by the hair.

'Shut up,' he said, and punched him hard in the face, as somewhere in the background a faint ringing sound began . . .

Alexei sat bolt upright in bed, stifling a shout of horror. To his immense relief, he saw that he was back in his uncle's apartment. His mobile was chirruping insistently on his bedside table; Alexei reached over and picked it up.

'Yeah?'

'You still sleeping, you lazy bastard?' a voice replied gleefully. Still recovering from his nightmare, it took Alexei a couple of seconds to work out it was Marat speaking. 'Put some clothes on and come and meet me. We've got work to do.'

Alexei wearily rubbed the sleep from his eyes. 'OK,' he said. 'Give me an hour.'

Reluctantly he hauled himself from the warm haven of his bed, pulled on a sweatshirt and padded barefoot towards the kitchen, relishing the smell of warm porridge floating towards him. Alexei had been prepared to spend another night in the monastery, but to his surprise Trojan had sent him home. Maybe it was a reward for taking part in the Eagles' ambush – maybe it was just to stop Stepan from asking more questions. It was never easy to tell with Trojan. One thing was for sure: after two days in the unsavoury company of the Moscow Eagles, it was great to be back in familiar surroundings.

Stepan had taken up his usual position by the stove, where he was carefully tending to the kasha. He gave his nephew a cool stare as he entered the kitchen, ignoring Alexei's cheery greeting.

'That haircut university policy?' said Stepan, pointing at Alexei's skinhead with a wooden spoon.

Alexei rubbed his head ruefully. 'It wasn't my idea. A couple of guys from the course thought it'd be a laugh if we all shaved our heads.'

'I see.' Alexei's uncle began stirring the porridge vigorously. 'Did they also think it would be funny to get involved in a punch-up?'

Alexei glanced guiltily down at his swollen purple knuckles. 'It was just training, uncle!' he protested. 'Sparring got a bit out of hand.'

'You look like a thug after a bar-room brawl,' Stepan said coldly. 'You'd better grow your hair back before your mother sees you. I'll be the one who gets into trouble for it, mark my words.' For a second Stepan had once again become the forbidding military man Alexei remembered from his childhood. Then his uncle relented, and said in a softer voice: 'Sit down and have some breakfast. You look tired. Any news of Lena?'

Alexei shook his head dumbly, sat down and began guiltily spooning the porridge into his mouth. It was the first time he had thought about Lena for an entire day. There was so much whirling round in his head that it was difficult to keep on top of everything. Still, that was no excuse, Alexei said to himself sternly, making a mental note to visit the hospital as soon as he had finished with Marat.

After breakfast, he showered and pulled on a tracksuit, covering his skinhead with a baseball cap. Telling Stepan he was going out training, Alexei headed out into the city. Marat was waiting for him in the main hall of Okhotny Ryad metro station, idly flicking through a tabloid as he leaned against the railings. A photograph of Rozalina Petrova was splashed across the front cover, underneath the headline 'LAWYER STILL ON DEATH ROW: 5 DAYS LEFT'.

Alexei nodded at the front page. 'I see everyone's still going on about that woman,' he said. 'She was the one who put Borovsky away, wasn't she?'

'Bitch,' muttered Marat. 'She'll get what she deserves.'

'You think?' Alexei asked. He paused. 'Or you know?'

Marat pointedly folded up the newspaper and tossed it on to a nearby bench. 'I wouldn't know about that,' he said, with icy deliberateness. 'I only read the paper for the football, anyway.'

In silence he led Alexei on to a train heading south on the Red Line. Marat refused to say where they were going, clearly relishing being in charge. Alexei had the feeling that the other teenager was something of a loner – he didn't command the respect that Viktor or Pavel generated, or the fear that greeted Medved's every appearance. If anything, the opposite was true: the rest of the Eagles often seemed to be mocking Marat. At least taking Alexei under his wing allowed Marat to feel more like a leader.

They finally got out at Universitet station, far to the south-west of the city. Hurrying under slate-grey skies, they made their way to the top of Sparrow Hills, every step revealing more and more of Moscow's skyline: Novodevichy Convent; Luzhniki Stadium; the sweep of the Moscow River as it curved through the capital. But Alexei's attention was focused squarely on the building looming up in front of him.

Moscow State University looked more like a giant cathedral than a place of learning, a towering construction rising hundreds of metres into the air. Two huge wings flanked a central tower, topped by a soaring spire with a Russian star that must have weighed tonnes by itself. The university, Alexei knew from his schooldays, had been one of a group of enormous Moscow skyscrapers known as the Seven Sisters. They had all been built under the orders of Josef Stalin, who wanted to dwarf New York's Empire State Building. As Alexei trudged up a broad, tree-lined avenue, the building seemed to grow ever larger and more intimidating, until the crowds of students milling around its entrance looked little more than ants.

'Didn't think you were the student type,' Alexei murmured to Marat.

'Ha ha,' the Eagle replied sarcastically. 'If anyone asks, we're visiting my cousin, right?'

They passed through a row of giant neo-classical pillars and entered the university lobby. As he looked around at the knots of students laughing and joking, Alexei couldn't help but be reminded that this was where he had planned to come and study in the autumn, before Lena had been attacked and his world had been turned upside down. Alexei wondered whether this would be the closest he would ever get to being a student here.

Marat led him through a marble hall and up a grand staircase, before following a path through a maze of long corridors and smaller flights of steps. He didn't pause once – this obviously wasn't the first time he had come here. Finally reaching the end of one of the corridors, the boy banged loudly on a door, not waiting for a response before opening it. Following him inside, Alexei stopped and stared.

They had entered a cramped student bedroom, where only a narrow stretch of red carpet separated the bed from a work desk. The walls were dominated by bookshelves and a corkboard plastered with photographs. Pale light slanted in through the open windows across the figure of a girl sitting reading on her bed. She was slim and in her late teens, her blonde hair trimmed into a neat bob. She looked up shyly as the boys entered her room.

'Alexei, this is Nadia,' Marat said proudly. 'She's responsible for our internet content. Thanks to her, people across the world have heard of the Moscow Eagles.'

Nadia smiled at Alexei, who was too surprised to do more than nod back. It was fair to say that she didn't look like any of the other Eagles he had met. Nadia put down her book and went over to her desk, where she opened her laptop.

'What have you got for me?' she asked.

Marat pulled a memory stick out from his pocket and tossed it on to her desk. 'Another classic Moscow Eagles' production,' he said proudly. As Nadia inserted the memory stick into her laptop, he explained to Alexei: 'Svetlana films our fights, and Nadia uploads them on to the internet. So you see, even though girls cannot fight alongside the Eagles, they can still help us in our struggle.'

They pulled up chairs next to Nadia and watched as she began to play the footage. Suddenly they were back outside the Uzbek cafe, watching from a distance as the Moscow Eagles charged. Alexei had seen videos of himself fighting in kickboxing tournaments, but that was sporting competition. This was something much worse. Watching now, he could see the shock and fear on the Uzbeks' faces as the Eagles came out of nowhere to attack. Sickened, Alexei saw himself throw a punch.

Nadia watched the footage expressionless. As she began transferring the file on to her hard drive, Marat boasted to her about his role in the fight. The way he told it, he had been leading the charge single-handed. Nadia laughed politely in the right places, but didn't encourage him. As the room fell quiet Marat got restless, and disappeared in search of a Coke.

Once the footage had transferred, Nadia clicked on an icon and logged on to a file-sharing program. Alexei watched as she began uploading the video.

'Isn't it a bit risky posting that on the internet?' he asked. 'I mean, the police can trace it back to you, can't they?'

'Not here,' Nadia replied. 'This is a darknet.' She laughed at his baffled expression. 'A private network linking users. It's anonymous and unmonitored – so you can email and transfer videos in complete privacy. It's tailor-made for the Eagles.'

'I didn't know you could do that.'

'It's pretty easy. All you need is the right software. People think they know about the internet, but they have no idea how big it actually is. Think of all the sites the search engines trawl – then times it by 500. That's a lot of shadowy corners.'

'How do you know all this?'

Nadia blushed. 'I like computers,' she said.

Sensing that the girl was beginning to relax, Alexei chatted to her about her course, seizing the opportunity to casually look around her room. Glancing up at the collage of photographs on the corkboard, he was surprised to see one of Nadia alongside Viktor Orlov. The leader of the 88s had his arm draped around her shoulders; the pair of them were laughing.

Nadia stopped talking mid-sentence as her mobile rang. She pulled a face as she checked the caller identity. 'My grandmother,' she explained. 'If I don't answer she'll end up calling the police or something.'

She slipped outside, leaving Alexei alone in the room. As he watched the video continue to upload on to the darknet site, a new email flashed up on the screen. It was from Viktor. Hurriedly checking the coast was clear, Alexei opened it. The message consisted of two curt sentences:

> Inform Tsar: the package is ready for delivery. Open the fortress gates.

Alexei frowned. Who the hell was Tsar?

'What are you doing?'

Alexei whirled round to see Nadia standing in the doorway.

'That's a private email,' she said angrily. 'Why are you looking at it?'

'I thought the video had finished transferring,' Alexei apologized hurriedly. 'I was trying to play it again but I guess I clicked on the wrong button. Sorry.'

Catching sight of the message, Nadia's face paled. She hurriedly closed her laptop.

'You should be more careful,' she said softly. 'People who make those kind of mistakes around the Eagles tend to get hurt.'

'We're dangerous people to be around,' Alexei replied. He held her arm. 'Makes you wonder why someone like you would hang around with us.'

Before Nadia could reply, Marat burst back into the room.

'Are we done yet?'

Nadia pulled out the memory stick and handed it back to Marat. 'I'll take it from here. The video will be up within the hour.'

'Better had,' said Marat, jokingly wagging a finger at her. 'I'll be checking!'

'It was nice to meet you,' Alexei added.

Nadia smiled, but as she closed the door behind them, her face was shaded with doubt.

'Nice girl, eh?' leered Marat, clapping Alexei on the back. 'Don't get any ideas, though, my friend. You got into enough trouble over Svetlana, and Nadia's a whole new level of danger, believe me.'

Alexei left the university in a state of bewilderment. He had been prepared for dealing with men like Marat and Medved, but Nadia had completely thrown him. What on earth was she doing?

He was sure of one thing, though: whatever that message had meant, judging by the look on Nadia's face, it was important. Alexei had no idea who Tsar was, or where the fortress was, but he had a strong hunch what the 'package' was: Rozalina Petrova. When the message was added to Marat's suspicious behaviour at Okhotny Ryad, Alexei was more convinced than ever that the Moscow Eagles were responsible for the lawyer's disappearance. Walking back through Universitetskaya Square, Alexei felt a first small surge of triumph.

12. Victory Park

As the metro train thundered through the tunnel back towards the centre of Moscow, Alexei struggled to hide his impatience. He had spent as much time in Marat's company as he could stomach, and he was desperate to contact Trojan. However, aware that he needed the Eagle as an ally, Alexei feigned interest as Marat babbled excitedly about football. It turned out that the only thing the teenager cared about more than the 88s was CSKA Moscow, and the big game with local rivals Dynamo was only two days away.

Suddenly, Marat fell silent mid-sentence, a look of hatred breaking out over his face like a storm cloud. Two young Georgian girls passed them in the carriage, their arms linked as they gossiped with one another. As they sat down, they looked over at Marat and Alexei and giggled coyly. Alexei's heart sank.

'Bitches!' spat Marat, clenching his fist. He tried to stand up, but Alexei grabbed his arm and pulled him back into his seat.

'Not here,' he said softly.

'Why not?' hissed Marat. 'They're laughing at us!'

Alexei glanced around the carriage, his mind racing as

he tried to think of a reason. 'Check out the guy behind us,' he muttered. 'I think he's a cop. He's packing a weapon under his jacket.'

Marat looked back at the middle-aged man leafing through a newspaper. 'Him? You reckon?'

Alexei nodded. 'Saw it when he got on the train. Let this one go – there'll be other opportunities.'

For a second it looked as though Marat was going to argue, but then he nodded sullenly. Alexei thanked his lucky stars it had only been the pair of them on the train – if Medved had been around, there would have been no restraining them. He dreaded to think what might have happened to the Georgian girls then. As Marat continued to gaze hatefully across the carriage, Alexei wondered whether this was how things had happened with Lena: a tiny spark setting off a sudden explosion of violence. Had Marat been there then, too? His mood darkening, Alexei was glad when they finally got off the train.

Back at Okhotny Ryad station, Marat tried to persuade Alexei to hang out with him for the rest of the day, but Alexei made his excuses and left. He waited until he was sure that the Eagle was out of sight, then pulled out Darius Jordan's business card from his pocket. Tapping the American's mobile number into his phone, Alexei texted him requesting a meeting. He had barely put down his phone when he received a reply:

Victory Park. 1500 hrs.

1455 hours: Alexei emerged from the metro and hurried

up a broad paved boulevard towards Victory Park. A memorial to Russia's struggles during World War Two, the vast park was built on top of Poklonnaya Hill, one of the highest points in Moscow. Alexei knew his way around: on his first weekend in the capital, Stepan had insisted on taking his nephew and Lena around the museum, his arms waving as he talked them passionately through the exhibits.

A caustic wind whipped across the boulevard, troubling the fountains that lined the route. It was bitingly cold. In front of Alexei, a soaring obelisk pierced the sky. A statue of Nike, the Greek goddess of victory, stared down impassively from its summit, over 140 metres into the air. Alexei felt dwarfed by the obelisk's solemn shadow.

Despite the unforgiving weather, Alexei had to thread his way through a bustling crowd of people: excitable schoolchildren, ignoring the stern commands of their teacher; foreign tourists, their faces glued to digital cameras; and ordinary Muscovites chatting to one another on the benches. Roller-skaters zoomed lazily through the throng, while in one corner of the park a pack of skateboarders were rattling down a set of steps. Irrationally, Alexei found himself looking out for members of the Moscow Eagles – as though any of the neo-Nazis would spend an afternoon paying their respects at a war memorial.

As Alexei came out on to the circular plaza at the obelisk's base, he glanced at his watch. It was 1500 hours. Where was Darius Jordan?

'Alexei.'

Suddenly, the head of Trojan Industries was by his

side, as though he had materialized out of thin air. The American was dressed in a heavy fur-lined coat, a pair of white earphones poking out from beneath a grey beanie hat.

'Where did you come from?' asked Alexei. 'I didn't see you.'

'You do now,' the American replied enigmatically.

'How's Lena?'

'Stable. There's been no improvement.'

'I should be with her,' Alexei said pensively. 'She needs me.'

'She needs you to complete her mission. If her condition changes you'll be the first to know. I've given you my word.'

As they walked slowly around the plaza, Alexei could see the other visitors openly staring at the tall, dark-skinned American. Westerners were not an everyday sight in Moscow – let alone men who looked like Darius Jordan. But if he was aware of the curious inspections, Jordan didn't show it. Alexei had never been around anyone who had exuded such calm self-confidence – except perhaps his father.

Jordan pointed at the crescent-shaped building that curved around the back edge of the plaza. 'Before you arrived, I took the opportunity to go round the museum. It's pretty incredible. Do you know how many Russians died during World War Two?'

'About twenty-five million,' Alexei replied automatically. He smiled wryly. 'Too many soldiers in the family. It's not the kind of fact they let me forget.'

'*Twenty-five million*. Jesus, Alexei! All those deaths, all those sacrifices just to stop the Nazis, and now, sixty years later, Russian kids are heiling Hitler and saluting swastikas.' Jordan shook his head. 'It baffles me.'

'You have racists in America, too,' Alexei pointed out. 'It's everywhere. People are poor, they can't get a job, they want someone to blame. It's easy to pick on immigrants.'

Jordan raised an eyebrow. 'You telling me about racism, son?' He barked with laughter. 'Can't say you're wrong, though.'

He stopped at the base of the obelisk, where a stone statue depicted a man on horseback wielding a spear – St George, the patron saint of Moscow, slaying the dragon. To an impatient Alexei, it seemed that the American was more interested in a history lesson than learning about his mission.

'Any news on the lawyer?' he asked pointedly.

Jordan shook his head. 'The authorities are maintaining a firm line – they don't negotiate with terrorists. I can understand their point. If they let someone as dangerous as Borovsky go free, it sends out the wrong kind of signals. God knows who gets kidnapped next. Besides, we've got a man inside the police department, and he's informed us that finding Ms Petrova isn't exactly top priority.'

'What do you mean?'

'Over the years Rozalina Petrova's been fighting pretty hard to get certain assault cases classed as race-hate crimes. That tends to complicate matters – and some policemen are more interested in an easy life than getting justice. And maybe some of them don't *entirely* disagree with the Moscow Eagles anyway. Didn't you say that you saw policemen cosying up to Medved after the attack on the Uzbeks?'

Alexei nodded. 'Put it this way: he wasn't in handcuffs.'

Jordan sighed, and looked out across the park. 'Wish I could say that I was surprised,' he said. 'I've been around the world, and Moscow's no different from anywhere else. It doesn't matter what uniform you're wearing, or which side you're supposed to be on, there's only one rule: there are good men and there are bad men, and you sure as hell gotta know which are which.'

'There aren't any good men in the Moscow Eagles,' Alexei said darkly.

'Damn right,' the American replied. 'Which is why we need to break them up. It's up to us, Alexei: if we can't locate Rozalina Petrova in the next five days, she's a dead woman. So what have you got for me?'

In a low voice, Alexei told Jordan about his conversation with Marat, their trip to the university and meeting with Nadia. At the mention of Viktor's email, the American's brow furrowed.

'Tsar? Means nothing specific to me. It's sure not the handle of a second-in-command, though. Sounds like Viktor's reporting to *someone*. You know, since I started studying the Eagles I've had a nagging feeling that there was more going on here than met the eye. Take the gym – it's in Viktor's name, but we've checked his employment records and he hasn't worked for years. Someone had to buy it; someone who didn't want it made public. Problem is, the money trail doesn't seem to go anywhere. If this Tsar is funding the Eagles, he knows what he's doing.'

'Guess I should go and find Marat – see if I can get any more information out of him.'

Jordan shook his head. 'You've taken enough risks for one day. Don't push your luck. We'll run Tsar through some databases, see what we can come up with. Meantime, you take the night off.'

Alexei laughed humourlessly. 'Thanks, boss.'

'Don't mention it,' Jordan replied, refusing to rise to him. He paused. 'Oh – I nearly forgot. Richard Madison wants me to ask whether you're taking care of that bug of his.'

Alexei had completely forgotten that he was still carrying the miniaturized listening device around. Patting his wallet pocket, he felt the familiar outline of the metallic disc.

'Tell him it's safe,' he replied. 'I'm just waiting for the right place to use it.'

'He'll be a relieved man. I know he's Technical Support, but sometimes I think he worries more about his gadgets than his kids.'

Alexei looked surprised. 'He's got kids?'

'We are actual human beings at Trojan, you know,' Jordan said, his voice laced with amusement. 'We've got kids, husbands and wives. Some of us are even lucky enough to have particularly demanding girlfriends . . .' His voice trailed off. 'We don't take this work lightly, son.'

'I guess,' Alexei replied, uneasy at the sudden change

of mood. 'I'm heading back now. Are you going to the metro station?'

Jordan thrust his hands deeper into his pockets. 'I think I'm going to stay here for a while. This is the kind of place you shouldn't rush visiting. Stay in touch – and be extra careful from now on. The deeper you go, the more dangerous it's going to get.'

Alexei nodded briefly, then turned and walked away. Halfway down the boulevard, he looked back to see the American still standing alone on the windswept plaza, neck craned upwards as he stared at the statue of the victory goddess.

13. Assault Course

Take the night off, Jordan had said. Easy for him to say, Alexei thought to himself bitterly. Having been totally immersed in his mission for five days, it wasn't as though he could just go to the cinema and forget about everything. The ironic thought occurred to Alexei that almost everyone he knew in this city was from either Trojan Industries or the Moscow Eagles – and he certainly didn't want to spend any more time with the latter.

In the end Alexei spent a sombre couple of hours at Lena's side in the hospital, then returned to his uncle's flat for dinner. Stepan was in a convivial mood, knocking back glasses of vodka as he attacked a plate of beef stroganoff and dumplings. Sitting in their warm kitchen, listening to Stepan's tales of youthful misbehaviour as the deep aroma of their meal swirled up around them, Alexei felt the first knots of tension in his shoulders begin to ease. Then his mobile phone buzzed in his pocket.

Assemble 0930 tomorrow at gym. Do not be late. Come prepared. V.

Alexei's heart sank. Come prepared for what? Another

street fight? He wasn't sure he could go through that again. He had just about managed to avoid doing any real damage last time, but the Eagles would be watching him now: he was certain of that. Even more unsettling was the fact that Viktor Orlov had his mobile number – presumably Marat had given it to him. Even though Alexei was trying to win the Eagles' trust, he didn't want to be any closer to their sinister leader than necessary. The fact that Viktor could contact him whenever he wanted bothered Alexei more than he could let on.

As he put his phone away, Alexei caught Stepan giving him an enquiring look over the rim of his vodka glass. 'Anything wrong, nephew?'

'Just more university stuff. It's no big deal.'

Stepan drained his glass and slammed it down on to the table. 'Maybe I'm just an old soldier,' he said, unscrewing the top off the vodka bottle, 'but this engineering course sounds distinctly fishy to me.' Suddenly there was an edge to his voice. 'Are you sure there's nothing you want to tell me?'

Alexei looked down at his food. Although part of him was desperate to confide in his uncle, he knew that Stepan would hit the roof if he heard the truth about Alexei's mission. Wartime heroics were one thing, but teenage black ops were something entirely different. Stepan would be on the phone to Alexei's parents in a heartbeat, and who knew what would happen then. What would Trojan do to keep their activities a secret – would Valerie Singer come knocking on their door again, this time with a gun in her hand?

Alexei shook his head. 'No. Thanks, though.'

His uncle harrumphed, and refilled his glass. The warmth had ebbed from the atmosphere in the kitchen, and they finished their meal in awkward silence. Stepan polished off his bottle of vodka in front of the television, getting so drunk that Alexei had to help him to bed. Next morning, as Alexei quickly showered and dressed, the apartment reverberated to the sound of his uncle's snores.

Any brief relief Alexei had felt the previous evening had been replaced by a sense of impending dread that only grew as he neared the Eagles' gym. He arrived just before half past nine to see the skinheads clambering into three white vans parked at the pavement. There had to be nearly thirty men in total – twice the size of the group who had attacked the Uzbeks.

Pavel was standing in front of the lead van, dressed purposefully in crisp combat fatigues. He broke off from shouting orders at the gang as Alexei approached, and glanced meaningfully at his watch. 'Just in time,' he said. 'Don't think we were going to wait for you.'

'What's going on?'

'No questions. Get in.'

Pavel gestured curtly at the third van and turned his back on Alexei. Trying to ignore the anxious feeling in the pit of his stomach, Alexei jogged over to the vehicle and jumped inside. The dingy confines were crammed with skinheads, none of whom Alexei recognized. The van reeked of body odour and bad breath. Deafening thrash metal pounded out from the car stereo at the front of the van, where Medved was hunched in the front seat, his hands drumming on the steering wheel. Alexei had barely taken his seat when someone slammed the van door shut, and they were moving.

It was impossible to be heard above the music, and no one was going to ask Medved to turn it down, so the men kept their own counsel as the van made its way north through the Moscow suburbs. Alexei almost wished that Marat was with him – at least they knew each other. He tried to ask a bullet-headed teenager where they were going, but the boy scowled and refused to answer.

Finally the van came to a stop. Alexei hurriedly opened the doors and leaped down on to the sunlit road, pleased to be out in the fresh air. He was standing on a quiet street in the shadow of a large, unfinished building – a forbidding complex of slate-grey levels, with black holes where the windows should have been. Even from this distance, Alexei could see the gaps in the walls where the concrete had crumbled away.

As he looked on, Marat climbed down from the second van and jogged over to him.

'Alexei!' the blond-haired boy hailed cheerily. 'Thought you weren't going to make it.'

'What's the big deal? What are we doing here?'

Marat jerked a thumb at the building. 'Training day.'

Alexei tried not to let the relief show on his face: training, he could handle. He followed the gang as they entered the complex grounds and snaked their way through an untamed forest of Japanese knotweed. Judging by the height of the plants, construction here on what was apparently going to be a hospital must have been halted several years ago. The Eagles reached the edge of the knotweed, and scrambled inside the building through a yawning hole in the wall.

Even in the dingy half-light of the interior, it was clear that the hospital was in a terminal condition. The floor was riddled with holes, and the gang had to skirt around piles of rubble as they made their way up to the roof of the complex. Water streamed through the ceilings and down the walls. Reinforcing rods poked out of the concrete as they vainly tried to keep the structure from falling apart. Everywhere Alexei looked, the walls were daubed with Nazi slogans and the Eagles' tag.

By contrast, the roof was bathed in warm spring sunshine. Viktor Orlov stood by the edge of the roof, dressed smartly in a full-length leather coat, dark trousers and a pair of sunglasses. Skinheads were changing into combat fatigues around him, against the bright-blue backdrop of the Moscow skyline.

Amid the heaps of green camouflaged rucksacks and multipacks of bottled water, Alexei was surprised to see Nadia sitting on a fold-up chair, her blonde hair tucked behind her ears and her brow creased in concentration as she typed at a laptop. Glancing up from the screen, she caught Alexei's eye: he gave her a friendly smile, but she immediately looked away. He still wasn't sure whether she had believed his story about the email back at the university – and whatever her relationship was with Viktor, Nadia certainly had his ear. As Alexei struggled into a set of musty fatigues with the rest of the gang, the leader of the 88s went over to place his hands on Nadia's shoulders, fondly kissing the top of her head as he inspected her screen. Then he clapped his hands together.

'Gentlemen!' Viktor called out. 'We stand alone at the front line of a war, my brothers: the true army of the White Russian. An army needs to be fit. An army needs to be lean. Days like today – tests like these, tests of the body and of the heart – are crucial if the Eagles are to be ready for war. We will be watching you, brothers. Do not disappoint us.'

Although his words echoed sonorously around the deserted complex, Alexei noticed that Viktor had made no moves to put on fatigues himself. Instead the leader of the Eagles took a seat alongside Nadia, allowing Pavel to step forward.

'You will all complete one full lap of the terrain with a rucksack on your back,' the ex-soldier said briskly. 'I will lead the way. Fifty press-ups for anyone who fails to keep up. There is no room for passengers in the 88s.'

Trooping over to pick up a rucksack, Alexei was astonished by how heavy it was. He unzipped it, only to see that the sack had been filled with bricks.

'What the hell –?'

There was an unpleasant laugh next to him. 'You're with men now,' growled Medved, slipping his rucksack on to his back as though it was filled with feathers. 'Try and keep up.'

Gritting his teeth, Alexei pulled on the rucksack. There was no way he was going to let Medved get a cheap laugh at his expense. The Eagles fell in line behind the diminutive form of Pavel, who turned and began jogging along the rooftop. Alexei took up a position close behind Medved at the back of the formation, trying to ignore the bricks scraping against his back as he kept pace with the giant skinhead. The air rumbled with the sound of boots clumping across the concrete.

The Eagles jogged down a set of steps running around the outside of the complex to the ground, before abruptly turning into a basement. Temporarily blinded by the plunge from sunlight to complete darkness, Alexei cried out as he felt his feet go out from under him and he tumbled into a pool of water. It was collected snowmelt – so cold that the air was buffeted from Alexei's lungs, and his heart pounded in protest. Weighed down by his rucksack, he desperately searched out a footing on the rocky floor, breaking back through the surface of the water. As Alexei wiped his eyes, gasping for breath, he saw the burly figure of Medved wading past him. The Eagle had completely ignored him. Alexei splashed angrily after him, and dragged himself out of the snowmelt on to dry land.

He soon realized that he was probably safer in the freezing pool. The basement was a pitch-black deathtrap of missing steps, holes in the floor, and reinforcement rods sticking treacherously out of the ground. It may have only been a training day, but there was real risk of serious injury here. The Eagles' pace slowed as they stopped to warn one another about the upcoming hazards. Still shivering from his plunge into the snowmelt, Alexei dropped to the back of the line.

As the basement exit finally came into view, there was a howl of pain in the gloom ahead of him. Peering through the darkness, Alexei saw that Medved had trapped his foot in one of the treacherous potholes, and was clutching his ankle in pain. Trying to suppress a grin of triumph, Alexei made to jog past him – only to stop in his tracks. Medved may have been a loathsome individual, but that didn't mean Alexei had to be too. He turned back and held out his hand. The large man looked up at him suspiciously, then grasped Alexei's hand and allowed himself to be hauled to his feet.

'You all right?' Alexei asked.

Medved gave him a furious look, checking Alexei's face for any sign of mockery. Eventually the large man nodded. 'Better get a move on,' he growled. 'Unless you like press-ups.'

Alexei didn't need the encouragement. As he burst out of the cellar back into the sunlight, leaving the hobbling Medved far behind, Alexei's competitive nature took over. He drove onwards through the vegetation and then back up through the levels of the hospital, taking pleasure every time he overtook a panting skinhead. The Eagles might have done this exercise before, but Alexei had been in intensive training of his own for years, and was nearing his physical peak.

By the time he had completed a circuit of the complex, only five of the Eagles had finished ahead of him. Alexei threw down his rucksack and peeled off his combat jacket, which was now drenched in a combination of sweat and snowmelt. As he took a couple of deep swigs from a water bottle, he was aware of Nadia closing her laptop down and rising from her chair.

'Not bad,' she said, with a faint smile.

'Thanks very much,' Alexei panted. 'I didn't see you down there.'

Nadia pulled a face. 'It's bad enough that Viktor makes me come and watch, without having to swim through freezing water in a dingy basement myself. Anyway, the Moscow Eagles don't let women take part in their army training.'

'But they don't mind you posting their videos of their "army training" afterwards,' Alexei shot back, rather more sharply than he had intended.

A shadow crossed Nadia's face; but before she could reply Viktor appeared at her shoulder. The blonde girl shrank away, returning to her chair and opening her laptop without another word.

'Well then, my young troublemaker!' Viktor declared expansively, leading him away from the rest of the gang. 'How did you find that?'

'OK,' Alexei replied cautiously. 'I was glad to get out of that basement.'

Viktor smiled, gracefully inclining his head. 'All in all, it was a most impressive display for a first time. But being a soldier is about more than fitness, Alexei. An army does not jog to victory. It fights; it kills.' He leaned in close, and whispered in Alexei's ear. 'When the call to arms sounds, do you think you could press the trigger?'

Goose-pimples broke out across Alexei's skin like bushfire. 'I don't – I don't know,' he faltered.

Viktor reached into the pocket of his leather jacket and pulled out a black semi-automatic pistol. He pressed the weapon into Alexei's hand. 'Only one way to find out,' he said quietly.

14. Burn Unit

The Eagles' shouts of exertion faded into the background as Alexei stared at the gun.

'What do you want me to do with this?' he asked quietly.

'I want you to fire it at Pavel.'

Alexei looked over at the ex-soldier, who was watching the last of the gang complete the course with a look of disdain on his face. Unlike the rest of them, who were spreadeagled out across the concrete, exhausted, there was barely a bead of sweat on Pavel's forehead.

'I don't understand,' Alexei said.

Viktor's face was solemn. 'What is there to understand? Are you questioning a direct order?'

'No . . . I'm not questioning . . .' stuttered Alexei. 'I just . . . Why do you want me to kill Pavel?'

Viktor gazed at him levelly through his horn-rimmed spectacles, then suddenly erupted into mocking laughter. 'Fear not, my young soldier,' he laughed. 'White Russia will not regain its pre-eminence by turning on its own. I don't want you to kill Pavel – but I do want you to shoot at him.'

At the sound of his name, the wiry man walked over

towards them. Viktor tossed him the weapon. 'Reassure our skittish young friend that this gun isn't going to kill anyone.'

'Frightened of this?' Pavel said scornfully. 'It's a child's toy.'

Taking aim at one of the large water bottles by the edge of the roof, he fired off several rounds almost negligently. Viktor waited until Pavel had emptied the chamber, then walked over and picked up the bottle, tipping it to one side. Water trickled out through small holes in the plastic where the pellets had penetrated the bottle. Pavel may have dismissed the gas-powered gun as a child's toy, thought Alexei, but getting hit was still going to hurt.

Viktor waited until the Eagles had caught their breath and collected themselves into a circle, then proclaimed in a ringing voice: 'Today is an auspicious day indeed, my brothers! To celebrate his entrance into the brotherhood of the 88s, Alexei has agreed to take on Pavel in a duel!'

Amid a murmur of excitement among the skinheads, Nadia gave Alexei a nervous look that did nothing to reassure him. As the entire gang headed down towards a lower level, Alexei could feel his heart thundering against his ribcage. He had never fired a gun in his life, and Pavel had been to war in Chechnya. It wasn't even going to be a contest.

Viktor brought them to a halt three floors down, in the middle of a vast space broken up by chipped pillars. The floor had bowed at the far end of this dilapidated arena, creating a depression in which a large pool of snowmelt had collected. The Moscow Eagles arranged themselves along one wall while, at Viktor's insistence, Alexei put on another layer of combat fatigues and strapped a ski mask over his face. The gun felt unfamiliar and heavy in his hand. Pavel had taken up a position directly facing him, a dark, sinewy silhouette against the sunlight pouring in through the window space behind.

'Ready?' Alexei said, trying to stop his hands trembling.

Viktor tapped the side of his face with a slender finger. 'Not quite yet,' he murmured. 'Let's make this a little more interesting. Marat!'

The blond-haired boy stepped forward almost apologetically, carrying a clear plastic water bottle. He began sprinkling liquid over Alexei's shoes and down his back.

'Hey!' Alexei protested. 'What the hell are you doing?'

'Stop moving!' hissed Marat. 'You don't want me to get this in the wrong place.'

Alexei caught a sniff of the acrid liquid. It wasn't water. It was lighter fluid.

'Are you crazy?' he yelled at Viktor. 'You're not setting me on fire!'

The leader of the Eagles stepped forward, his face serious. 'What did I tell you before we started? Today isn't just a test for the body, Alexei. It is also a test for the heart.' Viktor pressed his hand against Alexei's chest. 'For us to trust you, you have to trust us, yes?'

At that moment, surrounded by violent skinheads in a deserted building, Alexei wasn't sure he had a choice. He nodded, not trusting his voice to hide his fear. Viktor clapped him on the back.

'Good boy.'

Someone stepped forward with a burning rag. Viktor lit Alexei's shoes and back, then stepped quickly away. Alexei felt the flames licking hungrily against his clothes.

'Three!' began Viktor. 'Two! One! Fire!'

Diving to one side, Alexei caught a glimpse of Pavel raising his gun and taking aim, sending a shot narrowly over his shoulder. The crowd was roaring – who for, he couldn't tell. Alexei was moving on instinct, ducking in and out of the pillars, firing wild shots in the direction of his opponent.

He felt a sharp stinging pain in his thigh, and then another: Pavel had found his range. Alexei wanted to shoot back, but the fire was scrambling his senses and he had no idea where his opponent was. Instead Alexei ducked behind a pillar, even as another pellet ricocheted off the edge of the concrete post. The flames were billowing up his combat fatigues.

'Hey!' Alexei shouted. 'Someone help me!'

Maybe his voice was muffled by the ski mask, but no one stepped forward to aid him. The roars of the Eagles were still echoing loudly around the level.

A pellet bit into the pillar millimetres above his head. Alexei didn't care about the duel now – all he wanted to do was to put the flames out. His fatigues had been consumed by fire, and his skin was screaming in protest. Dropping his gun, Alexei began rolling around on the floor, but the flames were now too fierce to be smothered. Alexei cried out in panic, but still no one came to his aid.

Staggering to his feet, Alexei ran over to the pool of snowmelt and dived headlong into the icy water. There was a loud sizzling sound, and a cloud of steam rose up from the pool. As he lay beneath the surface, soaking his singed skin, all Alexei could hear was the scornful laughter of the Moscow Eagles.

From his vantage point on a low roof to the east of the complex, Alexei stretched out stiffly and watched as two small figures abseiled down the main wall of the hospital. The skin on his back was still tender from where the fire had taken hold, and the stench of smoke lingered on his clothes and in his nostrils.

He was grateful to be on his own – in particular, that Viktor and Pavel were somewhere down among the Japanese knotweed, overseeing the abseiling. Following the duel, the Eagles' leader had graciously suggested that Alexei sit out the afternoon's activities. Alexei agreed only too readily, not caring any more what the gang thought of him. If he had hoped that taking part in such a dangerous duel would have gained him credibility, he had been sorely mistaken. The rest of the Eagles seemed to find the incident funny – Alexei had a sneaking suspicion that humiliating him had been the whole point of the duel. Only Nadia showed any concern, gravely handing Alexei a couple of icepacks as he walked gingerly back up to the roof. She left the complex soon afterwards, parting with a final enigmatic glance in Alexei's direction.

Slow footsteps sounded behind Alexei; a hipflask was thrust under his nose. Medved was standing over him.

Alexei waited for a triumphant or nasty remark, but instead the large man waved the flask under his nose again. Cautiously, Alexei took a swig, and felt burning liquid drip down his throat. He wiped his mouth with the back of his hand and passed the flask back.

'Thanks,' he said. 'How's the ankle?'

Medved shrugged. 'I've had worse.' He opened a pack of cigarettes. 'Smoke?'

'After today?' replied Alexei. 'I think I'll pass.'

The burly man nodded, then lit a strong-smelling cigarette. Alexei pointed at the abseilers as they continued to inch their way down the side of the hospital.

'I figured you'd be up with them,' he said.

Medved snorted. 'What the hell would I do on a rope?' He paused, taking a deep drag from his cigarette. 'Anyway, I don't like heights.'

'Piss off!' laughed Alexei.

'It's true.' Medved shot him a sideways glance. 'Tell anyone and I'll beat the shit out of you.'

Alexei held up his hands. 'Your secret's safe with me. Can't pretend I fancy it either. It's dangerous enough jogging round here, let alone hanging off the side of a building. This place is a dump.'

'Of course it's a dump,' said Medved. 'That's the whole point.'

'What do you mean?' Alexei asked cautiously.

'Say a hospital needs building, and a certain construction firm wins the contract to build it. Say this firm takes some shortcuts during construction – maybe the concrete isn't so good, so things start falling apart pretty quickly, and you end up with a half-built ruin like this. Still, the money the firm's saved gets shared around, and so nobody ends up complaining.' Medved flicked his cigarette end off the roof. 'It's a classic Construktko tactic,' he concluded.

'Construktko?' Alexei said, with a frown. 'The same guys whose site you raided last year?'

Medved nodded. 'Mr Lebedev – the owner – lets us use this place. Long as we don't advertise it, of course. Viktor says that –'

'Medved!'

The burly skinhead whirled round to see Viktor Orlov standing in the doorway behind him. The Eagles' leader briskly beckoned him away. Pretending to be engrossed in the abseiling, out of the corner of his eye Alexei watched as the two men engaged in a hushed conference on the other side of the roof. Viktor was angrily jabbing his finger at Medved, who received the tirade with surprising meekness. Eventually Viktor pushed the skinhead back towards the doorway and they went downstairs without saying another word to Alexei.

The sky was turning pink with the onset of evening before the training was completed. As the Eagles packed up their gear and headed back to the vans, Alexei saw that the day had had an impact on the gang members. At the beginning, the skinheads had been a mistrustful, surly group – now, bonded by the physical challenges, they patted each other on the back and helped one another with their gear. In one day, Viktor and Pavel had bred comradeship among their men.

Not that Alexei felt part of their gang. All day the Eagles had been playing games with him – whether to test him, or just humiliate him, Alexei couldn't be sure. He had had the last laugh, though. Clearly Medved had told him something he shouldn't. As Alexei sat in the back of the van as it rumbled back to Moscow, one question occupied his mind. Given that the Eagles had run riot through a site owned by Construktko, what on earth was its owner doing letting them train on his buildings?

15. Blood Rift

The next morning, Alexei woke up to find his uncle's apartment empty, and his clothes from the day before in a smoky pile in the corner of his room. He checked his mobile phone, and was relieved to find that there were no messages waiting for him. For the time being, he needed a break from the Moscow Eagles.

After a long shower, Alexei wrapped a towel around his waist and padded barefoot out of the bathroom and into the kitchen. He scanned the sparse contents of the fridge, pulled out a bottle of orange juice and took a deep swig. As he drank, a key rattled in the apartment's front door and Stepan shuffled into the kitchen, laden down with shopping bags.

'You wouldn't believe the trouble I had in the supermarket,' he began, placing the bags down on the table. 'The bloody woman at the checkout –'

He looked across at Alexei and stopped, his face paling.

'What the hell is that?' he whispered, pointing a trembling finger at his nephew's chest. Alexei looked down, and saw the swastika tattoo on his glistening skin.

'Wait!' he said urgently. 'It's not what it looks like . . .'

'It's a bloody swastika, Alexei!' yelled Stepan. 'It's

exactly what it looks like! What in God's name were you thinking? What do you think your mother and father would say if they saw that? What do you think *Lena* would say, Alexei? Have you even visited her recently?'

'You don't understand,' Alexei shot back. 'I did this for Lena!'

Stepan laughed incredulously. 'What kind of nonsense is that? You shave your hair off, you tattoo filth on your chest, and all this is for your girlfriend? What the hell is going on?'

Alexei's explanation died in his throat. How could he begin to explain what was going on?

'I can't tell you,' he said finally. 'I'm sorry.'

Stepan looked at his nephew for a long time, then shook his head sadly. 'No, I'm sorry,' he said. 'Pack your bags. You've been acting strangely ever since this "course" of yours started. I don't know what in hell is going on, but I can't allow it to take place under my roof. If you've got any sense remaining, you'll go back to Volgograd. If you won't talk to me, you'll have to talk to your parents.'

'You can't tell them, uncle!' pleaded Alexei. 'Give me a week at least!'

'You ask too much of me.'

'Just one week! Everything will be sorted by then, I promise!'

'How am I supposed to trust you if you won't tell me what's going on?'

Alexei clutched his arm. 'Because you know me. You know I wouldn't do something like this unless it was important. Lena would support me, I know she would;

can't you, too? Kick me out if you have to, but at least give me a week before you tell my parents. Please.'

His uncle looked away out of the kitchen window – then quickly nodded his head.

'One week,' he said. 'But don't even think about coming back here until that thing on your chest is gone.'

Stepan retreated to his room and closed the door, leaving Alexei to throw his clothes into a bag and walk out of the flat without even a goodbye. Alexei's head was light with disbelief – he couldn't quite believe his uncle had thrown him out. Where was he supposed to go? There only seemed to be one option.

Alexei made a forlorn journey across Moscow to the Taganka district. He was climbing up the hill towards Trojan's monastery when his phone began to ring. He pressed the answer button.

'Hello?'

'Alexei?' It was Richard Madison. 'What's going on, mate?'

'I'm coming up to the monastery. My uncle saw my Nazi tattoo and kicked me out. I need a place to stay.'

'Really sorry to hear that. I'm sure you'll be able to patch things up after your mission ends. But you need to walk past the monastery. You're in deep cover now. The less contact you have with us the better.'

'I've got nowhere else to go. I'm coming in.'

'Listen to me, Alexei.' Madison's voice was urgent. 'They're following you.'

Alexei stopped in his tracks. 'What did you say?'

'There's a couple of goons in a red Lexus keeping an

eye on you. If you start hanging out in a deserted monastery you can be sure that's going to get back to Viktor.'

Alexei had to force himself not to turn round and look for the car. How long had the Eagles been following him? Had they seen him visit Lena? 'Wait a second.' He frowned. 'How do you know this?'

'Because we're following you too. We've just had a little bit more practice than them. How do you think I knew you were coming to the monastery?'

Alexei rubbed his eyes wearily. 'So let me get this straight: my girlfriend's in the hospital, my uncle's thrown me out, I'm being followed, and now you guys won't help me. What do I do now – go and sleep on a park bench? Who the hell am I supposed to stay with?'

Madison told him.

'Oh, you've got to be kidding me,' Alexei said sourly.

He continued past the monastery's driveway without glancing at the building, plagued by dark thoughts. At that moment, it felt like the whole world was against him. Alexei was tempted to jump on a train and go back to Volgograd and the cosy familiarity of his parents' house, leaving Moscow and Trojan Industries and skinhead gangs far behind him. Only the thought of Lena – and the promise he had made at her bedside – kept him going.

As he waited at a busy crossing, Alexei glanced behind him and caught a sight of the Lexus parked on the other side of the road. A burly man was sat at the wheel, pretending not to watch him. There was no sign of anyone from Trojan. The fact that they were also watching him didn't comfort Alexei in quite the way it should have done.

Tired of walking, he climbed on to a crowded bus that was heading to the manufacturing district of Krasnoselsky. It was mid-afternoon by the time he reached his goal: a rundown apartment block next to an industrial estate. A gang of teenagers had gathered in the car park in front of the building, accompanied by a large Rottweiler. They stared at Alexei as he walked past them, while the dog snarled and strained at its leash.

On the second floor, he walked along the corridor and banged on a door halfway down it. The door opened, and Marat peered out suspiciously from behind it. He was bare-chested, revealing an array of white power tattoos. At the sight of Alexei, his face brightened.

'Alexei! What are you doing here?'

'Had a fight with my girlfriend,' Alexei replied dully. 'She kicked me out. Can I stay here for a bit?'

'Women,' said Marat, shaking his head. 'They're all bitches. Come in, my friend.'

He opened the door wide, and Alexei walked reluctantly into the skinhead's apartment.

It was worse when she was awake.

Rozalina Petrova had no idea where she was, or how long she had been held captive. She barely knew her own name. Her captors had drowned her system with drugs to keep her docile – not that she could have escaped even if she had been thinking clearly.

Her senses had been numbed to the point of unconsciousness, but she was still aware of certain things: the cold stone floor on her bare legs, the handcuffs biting into her wrist, the radiator digging into her back, the heavy metal music that pounded through the walls. In the brief interludes when the drugs wore off, as Rozalina peered around the dark surroundings, pangs of terror assailed her and she struggled to breathe. In some ways, it was a relief when they returned to inject her again.

Now she was dimly aware of bolts being slid back outside her cell door, and a masked man entering the room. All the gang members wore balaclavas when they were around her. The man pulled up a chair and sat down, leaning forward to inspect Rozalina so closely that she could smell the alcohol on his breath. He held her by the chin; sluggishly, she shied away.

The man laughed, then sat back and pulled up his balaclava. Even in her dazed state, Rozalina recognized him – it was Oleg, the man who had pretended to be a journalist. There was still something naggingly familiar about his face, even as it twisted into a hateful grin.

'Comfortable?'

She shook her head, trying to clear the cobwebs from her mind. 'Let . . . me . . . go,' she said slowly, making a great effort to frame the words.

'Aren't you having fun here?' the man asked mockingly.

'People will come looking. They will find me.'

'No, no, no,' he said, briskly shaking his head. 'Very safe here. Long way from Moscow. No one is going to stick their nose in.'

'People will find me,' Rozalina insisted. 'They have to.'

'Do you even think the police are looking for you? There are only four days before our deadline expires. If the authorities want to keep you alive, they have to free Nikolai Borovsky. Yet the police have barely asked us a question. We have many friends, Rozalina Petrova. Friends in powerful places who agree with our aims.'

As the man spoke, Rozalina suddenly remembered where she had seen him before. 'I know who you are,' she said. 'There was a photograph of you in Borovsky's case files. You're a Moscow Eagle too, aren't you? And your name isn't Oleg.' Rozalina frowned. 'Pavel someone?'

The man broke into a slow round of applause. 'Well done. Pity you didn't remember that before you let me into your car, you dumb slut.'

'It doesn't matter who you kidnap – they'll never release Borovsky.'

'Of *course* they're not going to free him!' Pavel exclaimed. 'But do you want to know a little secret?' He whispered behind the back of his hand. 'We don't give a shit. That was never the point.'

'Then why am I here?'

'You're here because we're going to wait until the deadline is reached, until all the media is focused on your whereabouts, and then . . . we're going to shoot you in the head.'

Rozalina's blood froze.

'Your execution,' continued Pavel, 'will serve as a powerful symbol to this country as to the fate of traitors like you – the Jews and the blacks who sully the name and glorious history of White Russia with their malignant presence. It will be the wake-up call to a generation. That will be your legacy.'

With that, Pavel leaned forward and jabbed a needle into her arm, pumping more drugs into her veins.

'Sweet dreams,' he whispered, planting a fetid kiss on her cheek.

Rozalina cried out, but her mind was already sinking back into the abyss, and by the time Pavel had walked out of her cell and slid the bolts back across her door, her eyes had gone glassy and her head sagged lifelessly to one side.

16. Bitter Rivals

Being in Marat's apartment was like being locked in a frozen cupboard. There was no furniture, only a sleeping bag laid out on a grubby mattress. A door half-hanging off its hinges revealed a cramped toilet beyond. The walls were covered in a dark sea of graffiti – a mixture of lewd drawings and racist slogans – while the ceiling had a giant swastika flag pinned to it. As he entered the room, Alexei nearly tripped over an electricity cable snaking across the floor, linking a battered CD player to the socket.

Judging by Marat's enthusiastic welcome, the young Nazi didn't get many guests. Alexei didn't even know if the skinhead had any family – it wasn't the sort of question to ask around the Moscow Eagles. After a few painful minutes sitting in silence Marat disappeared outside, returning with an armful of cheap beers. They spent the rest of the day sitting on his floor, necking the bottles.

Even though Marat boasted that he was one of the biggest drinkers in the gang, it wasn't long before he started to slur his words. He only had one topic of conversation: the Moscow Eagles. Whenever Alexei tried to change the subject, Marat quickly got bored, going off to the toilet or changing the CD. Listening to his drunken rants, and looking around the impoverished apartment, Alexei wasn't sure whether he really did hate Marat, or just pitied him.

Despite his low opinion of the company, Alexei was glad to be indoors. He drank quickly, desperate to forget the way things had turned out that day. But no matter how much beer he tipped down his throat, two things kept nagging away at him: the horrible, morbid fear that Lena was never going to wake up, and the fact that he only had four days left to find Rozalina Petrova. As Marat clumsily knocked the top off another bottle, drenching himself in foam in the process, Alexei decided to take a chance.

'You ever met this guy Tsar?' he asked casually.

'Never heard of him,' Marat replied. 'Why?'

'Just heard a couple of the Eagles talking about him. Sounded like a pretty important guy.'

'*Sounds* like something you shouldn't have been eavesdropping on,' countered Marat, his eyes narrowing. 'And what's with all the questions, anyway?'

'Hey, I didn't mean anything by it,' Alexei replied, taking another sip from his bottle. 'Just curious, that's all.'

'You're too curious,' Marat slurred. 'Can't you see the Eagles don't like it when people start asking questions? Why d'you think Viktor did all that shit to you at the training day? I told him, "Viktor, you can trust Alexei. I know him. He's one of us." But he's one suspicious bastard. He doesn't listen to me.'

This was bad news. It sounded as though Viktor was

on to him. If Alexei hadn't been sure he was on dangerous ground with the Moscow Eagles, he was now. Before he could try and get anything more from Marat, the skinhead put down his bottle and slumped out on the mattress. His mouth yawned like a cavern as he snored.

Alexei spent the longest night of his life huddled on the floor of Marat's apartment, his extra layers of clothing failing to ward off the cold. It was getting light by the time he finally fell asleep; he woke up what felt like seconds later with a throbbing headache and a sour taste in his mouth. He was vaguely aware of a toe poking him in the ribs.

'Piss off, Marat,' mumbled Alexei.

'Get up, you lazy black!' the skinhead crowed back. 'We've got things to do.'

'Like what?'

'You gotta ask me? CSKA are playing Dynamo today! I'm not missing that! Get up and let's go.'

Marat was in an irritatingly chirpy mood, apparently unaffected by all the beer they had drunk. As the alcohol drained from his system, Alexei felt dark clouds of doubt descending around him again; he got groggily to his feet and went and splashed some water on his face.

On their way through town, they stopped off at a fast-food restaurant; Alexei nearly gagged on his Coke as he watched Marat bolt down his burger meal. The prospect of the match did little to cheer him up. Back home, it had been Lena who had dragged him to watch Rotor Volgograd play – Alexei had spent many afternoons looking on wryly as his girlfriend lost herself in the game:

jumping up and down with excitement at every near miss; cursing loudly every time the opposition scored; chewing on her nails as the seconds counted down to a hard-fought victory. For her part, Lena could never understand how Alexei could remain so indifferent.

The CSKA game was taking place at Dynamo Stadium, a low-slung arena in the middle of Petrovsky Park. With Dynamo and CSKA both Moscow teams, and fierce rivals, the atmosphere outside the ground was as sharp as a Stanley knife, and rows of policemen in riot gear lined the roads leading up to the stadium. Alexei and Marat followed a group of men dressed in blue and red – CSKA's colours – through the turnstiles, and pushed their way to the back of the stand, where the team's hard-core Ultra fans had gathered. Most of the grim-faced men there seemed to recognize Marat, though a brisk nod was the warmest greeting he got. Alexei spotted a couple of familiar figures from the Moscow Eagles, despite the hoods pulled up over their heads and the scarves wrapped around the lower half of their faces. Even though Alexei wasn't much of a football fan, the tension in the ground made the hairs on the back of his neck prickle, and he joined in with the crowd's roar as the teams made their way on to the pitch.

'Watch this, Alexei,' Marat said, clapping. 'We're going to stuff these bastards. I just know it.'

Things went very wrong very quickly. After only five minutes, CSKA's marking fell to pieces at a corner, allowing Dynamo's giant centre-back to crash home a free header. The goal was greeted with oaths and dark mutterings from the Ultras. CSKA had barely kicked off before Dynamo's tricky winger jinked inside the full-back and curled a beautiful effort into the net. All around Alexei, people began jeering and hurling abuse; a couple of red flares were hurled on to the pitch in the direction of the CSKA goalkeeper. By half-time it was 3–0 to Dynamo, and the mood in the stands was turning violent. The Dynamo fans were gleefully taunting their rivals, who were straining at the wire fencing separating the two sets of supporters.

'Screw the game,' a man growled behind Alexei. 'We'll win the fight afterwards.'

There were growls of agreement, and a chant of 'Red! Blue! Warriors!' erupted across the stand. Beside Alexei, Marat remained silent. He seemed completely flattened by the scoreline.

'This is shit,' he muttered suddenly. 'I'm getting out of here.'

He elbowed his way out of the stand, ignoring the cold stares of the other Ultras. Alexei followed almost apologetically on his heels.

Outside the ground, the atmosphere was tightening like a garrotte. One of the policemen was struggling to keep control of an Alsatian, which was barking loudly at a group of CSKA fans gathering menacingly around the exits. Marat stormed past without a glance, walking in the opposite direction to the nearest metro station and into a maze of quieter streets flanked by large warehouses.

'Useless bastards!' The skinhead kicked out at an empty beer bottle, sending it smashing against a wall. 'Footballers are just like everyone else – they don't give a shit. All they care about is screwing us over.'

'It's just a game, Marat,' Alexei said.

Marat whirled round and grabbed two fistfuls of Alexei's shirt, his eyes wild. 'It's *not* just a game! It's important!'

For a second Alexei thought the boy was going to try and hit him, but Marat hesitated. Then, with a sound of irritation, he let go of Alexei and stalked away. Normally Alexei would have been happy to let him go, but he still didn't have anywhere else to stay and there was no way he was contacting Trojan again. Instead, he followed a safe distance behind Marat, hoping that the Eagle would eventually cool off.

Still audibly muttering to himself, Marat disappeared down a narrow alleyway that cut between two rundown factories. Alexei tracked him to the mouth of the passageway – and was nearly knocked off his feet by Marat, who was running headlong in the opposite direction.

'Run for it!' the skinhead shouted.

Alexei barely had time to react before a group of men came hurtling round the corner towards him. At first he thought they were Dynamo fans, but then he caught a glimpse of their faces, and realized it was much worse than that.

It was the Uzbeks the Eagles had assaulted in the street.

The lead man was on him in an instant: Alexei wrenched his left shoulder out of the way just in time, as a screwdriver slashed wickedly through the space it had been occupying. Grabbing the man's extended arm, Alexei moved inside and drove his knee into the man's crotch. As his assailant crumpled in pain, Alexei threw a couple of short rights at the man's head, and was moving away before he hit the ground.

Hearing a cry of alarm, he saw that two men had caught up with Marat, who was lashing out in a vain attempt to keep them at bay. Alexei raced over and punched one of the Uzbeks in the back of the head, knocking him to the floor. The second man whirled round, only to receive a powerful side kick in the ribs. He clutched at his side, winded, unable to protect himself from a flurry of clubbing punches from Marat.

Alexei looked back behind him, adrenaline coursing through his system. Although they had dealt with the first wave, more Uzbeks were sprinting towards them.

'We can't take all of them!' Marat shouted.

Not on open ground, they couldn't. Scanning the surrounding buildings, Alexei spotted a metal door standing slightly ajar.

'This way!' he shouted.

Half-dragging Marat behind him, Alexei crashed through the door, and into the unknown beyond.

17. Dead Meat

A thunderous rumbling overwhelmed Alexei. Blinking, he saw that he was standing at the edge of a factory floor, amid hulking steel machines that gleamed in the unforgiving illumination of the strip lights. Conveyor belts were ferrying lumps of raw meat into the machines' maws, where they were sliced and ground down. Lines of men dressed in white aprons and hats oversaw the frenzied feeding – even from this distance, Alexei could see that they all had Asiatic slants to their features.

Marat swore loudly. 'More of the bastards!'

'They're not the ones we have to worry about,' replied Alexei, nervously glancing back at the door. 'Come on!'

They ran across the factory floor, splashing through shallow pools of water. The workers barely looked up from their work as Alexei and Marat charged past them, their heads dutifully bowed as they concentrated on processing the meat. Behind them, the angry shouts of the Uzbeks carried above the machinery as they burst inside the building.

Alexei cut sharply left and then right, elbowing workers out of the way as he raced down a narrow aisle between one of the grinders and the far wall. With no exits in sight, he made towards a staircase leading up to a first-floor gangway and took the metal steps three at a time. Marat was hot on his heels, fearfully glancing back over his shoulder.

The wide gangway ran around all four walls, offering a view of the entire factory. Alexei crouched down and peered through the guardrail. The Uzbeks had fanned out across the floor below, warily scanning the aisles for their prey. It was only a matter of time before they turned their attention to the gangway.

'They're cutting off the exits!' Marat panted at his side. 'We'll never get out of here!'

As Alexei watched, one of the Uzbeks grabbed hold of a factory worker and shouted at him, gesturing wildly, but the man in the apron silently shook his head and returned to his work.

'At least the locals aren't talking,' Alexei remarked. 'We'll find a way out up here. But stay low, all right?'

They scurried round the gangway, past a row of long processing tables covered in giant slabs of meat. Thankfully, there were no workers on this level to impede their progress. Turning the corner of the walkway, Alexei caught sight of a door set into the far wall. If their luck was in, maybe there was a way out through there.

Alexei had covered half the distance when he skidded to a halt, triumph turning to despair like ashes in his mouth. Another processing table had obscured the fact that another staircase came out on to the gangway – and an Uzbek had just appeared at the top of it.

Startled, the youth tried to shout out a warning to his

companions, but the clanking machinery drowned him out. Instead he snatched up a meat cleaver from the nearest table and waved it threateningly at Alexei.

'He's got a blade!' cried Marat, backing away. 'Let's get out of here!'

'Where, exactly?' Alexei replied, through clenched teeth. 'We've got to get past him!'

The Uzbek slowly advanced upon them, the sharp edge of the cleaver glinting malevolently. Alexei assumed a fighting stance, trying to block out the noise and the mayhem surrounding him as he concentrated on his opponent. The youth twitched, and suddenly the cleaver was whistling through the air. But Alexei had already dropped to the ground, and with a low sweeping kick knocked his assailant to the floor. He leaped on top of the Uzbek, grabbed the hand holding the cleaver and repeatedly banged it against the metal gangway. With a howl of pain, the youth let go.

Alexei rolled to one side and drove his elbow into the Uzbek's face – heard a sickening crunch as he made impact. As the youth clutched at his face, Alexei pulled him to his feet and hurled him over the guardrail. The Uzbek screamed as he plummeted downwards, landing heavily on one of the conveyor belts. His bloodied face contorted with dismay as he was carried helplessly away on a sea of raw meat.

Before Alexei could catch his breath, a cry went up from one of the men on the factory floor. They had been spotted. Immediately the Uzbeks flocked towards the stairs.

Alexei turned around to see Marat still cowering by

the processing table. 'What are you waiting for?' he shouted. 'Move!'

He hared along the gangway and yanked open the door, entering a dingy toilet that flooded his nostrils with the smell of urine. Three cubicles stood side-by-side in front of him, next to a grimy washbasin that was only just managing to cling to the wall. There was no way out.

'Shit!' spat Alexei, kicking a bin.

Marat peered back outside through a crack in the door. 'They're coming!' he wailed. 'What the hell are we going to do now?'

In desperation, Alexei opened the first stall, and then the other. Inside the farthest cubicle, his heart leaped to see a small latched window set into the back wall. He hauled Marat inside the cubicle and locked the door, trying not to gag at the sludgy brown mess stagnating in the toilet bowl. Opening the window, Alexei looked down the three-metre drop to the street below. Marat dubiously followed his gaze.

'Big drop,' he said.

'Fine. You can stay and hang out with them if you want. I'm getting out of here.'

'All right, all right,' Marat said hastily. 'I'll go first.'

He unzipped his jacket and stuffed it through the window. Then, standing on the toilet, he climbed up to the window and tried to wriggle through it.

'Tight squeeze,' he muttered.

There came the sound of footsteps outside, and then the door to the toilets creaked ominously open. Marat's belt buckle had caught on the windowsill; the blond teenager scrabbled furiously as he tried to free himself.

Alexei could hear the men creeping into the toilet. There was a crash as the first stall door was kicked open.

'Hurry up!' Alexei hissed. With a final squirm, Marat slipped out through the window, tumbling down to the pavement below. Alexei dived after him, instantly wedging himself in the window frame.

He heard the second stall door fly open.

Wriggling violently, Alexei felt his skin tearing on the rough wooden frame. He didn't care any more: all he could think about was getting himself free. As the final stall door exploded open, Alexei wrenched himself through the narrow gap, and plunged headlong to the ground.

It didn't start to hurt until later. Picking themselves up from the pavement, Alexei and Marat had staggered blindly away from the meat factory, their only thought to put as much distance between themselves and their attackers as possible. Eventually Marat had stopped, wheezing heavily as he pulled out his mobile phone and dialled a number.

As a result of the ensuing conversation, Alexei now found himself standing at a quiet crossroads, digging his hands into his pockets as night fell. He had been waiting for over an hour, and the temperature was rapidly dropping towards freezing. The left side of his body ached from where he had hit the ground, and all he wanted to do was get inside in the warm and lie down, but Marat had insisted that they stay put. Having fallen to pieces in the factory, the blond teenager seemed intent on reasserting his authority.

It wasn't just the cold Alexei was worried about. He kept checking the intersection for any signs of danger. After all, if the Uzbeks had managed to track them all the way to the CSKA match, there was no reason why they couldn't pick up the trail again.

Shivering, he turned and gave Marat a reproachful look. The Eagle was perched dejectedly on the back of a bench, his feet resting on the seat.

'Whatever we're waiting for, it'd better be worth it,' griped Alexei. 'I'm freezing my balls off out here.'

'I was given an order,' Marat said stubbornly.

Alexei was about to tell the boy exactly where he could shove his order when a white van hurtled across the crossroads and screeched to a halt alongside them, its engine still running. Marat got down from the bench, jogged over to the back of the van and opened up the rear door. As he climbed inside, Alexei was surprised to see Viktor Orlov sitting calmly in the front passenger seat. Next to him, Medved had one hand on the steering wheel and another holding up his mobile phone, his massive fingers clumsily spelling out a text. As the skinhead pulled away from the side of the road in a cloud of exhaust fumes, the leader of the Eagles swivelled round to look at Alexei.

'Give me your report,' he said curtly. 'Leave nothing out.'

Alexei told him everything that had happened since the football match. Viktor listened intently, his gaze never straying from Alexei's face. After he had finished, the leader of the 88s thoughtfully pushed his glasses up the bridge of his nose.

'A close shave,' he said. 'The Uzbeks must have been watching you for a while, waiting for the moment to strike. I'm impressed that you managed to escape from the situation unharmed.'

'That was down to Alexei,' Marat confessed. 'If he hadn't been there, I'd have been screwed.'

'Really?' Viktor's eyes glinted in the darkness. 'Is that true?'

Alexei shrugged. 'We got out,' he said simply. 'Doesn't matter how.'

'Perhaps not,' Viktor agreed. 'But that doesn't mean I'm not grateful. The Eagles are brothers, Alexei – we have to take care of one another. Especially in the face of such a cowardly enemy.'

Medved angrily thumped the steering wheel. 'Those dirty Uzbek bastards!' he roared. 'I'm going to put some men together and end this!'

'You'll do nothing of the sort,' Viktor said sharply. 'Right now this is just a sideshow to other, more important matters. We *will* hold them to account, Medved, don't you worry. But not just yet.'

'So we do nothing?' the burly skinhead said bitterly. 'Sit on our asses and twiddle our thumbs?'

'Just because we choose not to fight tonight, doesn't mean we have to do nothing,' said Viktor. 'Our young friends here have proved the bravery of the white man in the face of greater numbers and a surprise attack. Surely that deserves something of a celebration?'

'Oh,' rumbled Medved. 'You mean Orbit?'

'Where else?' Viktor replied, with a smile.

18. Night Lights

The white van rattled down a broad floodlit street, passing a row of casinos drenched in cascades of sparkling lights. Impossibly beautiful faces stared down from giant adverts for films and perfumes. When they had first moved to Moscow, Lena had joked to Alexei that she was going to appear on a billboard in double-quick time, in order to keep an eye on him in the big city and make sure he was behaving himself. *When's your horror film coming out then?* he had quipped back, earning a sharp pinch on the arm for his troubles, and five minutes of angular silence until he had apologized.

Despite the fact he hadn't been here long, even Alexei had heard of Orbit. It was renowned as the most glamorous nightspot in Moscow – no small claim, in a city this hedonistic. Given that only the most well-to-do and fashionable Muscovites were allowed past Orbit's notoriously brusque bouncers, Alexei wondered exactly how the Eagles were planning to gain entrance. Only Viktor was dressed smartly enough to get in, while Alexei and Marat's clothes were stained and torn from their encounter in the meat factory.

'Shouldn't we go change or something?' Alexei asked, as Medved parked the van out of sight at the bottom of the street. 'There's no way they're going to let us in looking like this.'

'Alexei!' Viktor said chidingly. 'You're an Eagle! We can drink wherever we want!'

A queue of young people was snaking hopefully down the street from Orbit's entrance, forming a glittering landscape of sculpted hairstyles and designer clothes. To their amazement, the Moscow Eagles marched straight past them to the front door, where a well-built man with a shaved head and an earring was standing guard. As Viktor approached, the bouncer lifted up the red rope cordon and gestured for him to pass through. There were shouts of incredulity from the queue – although the wiser clubbers were careful to keep their protests to a mutter. Viktor smiled benignly at the shaven-headed man.

'Thank you, Dmitri.'

The bouncer nodded respectfully. As he replaced the rope cordon, Alexei noticed the number '88' tattooed in blue ink on the web of skin between the bouncer's right thumb and forefinger. Suddenly, everything became clear. As they swept straight through into the club, Alexei wondered how far Viktor's contacts stretched. How many doors were opened to him?

Orbit was a honeycomb of dingy rooms drenched in red strobe lights. Alexei passed through an archway into a large hall decked with drapes and baroque decorations. Even though it was early, statuesque women were already dancing to the thumping Eurobeat, their bodies moving sinuously in time with the music. Men watched admiringly from the side of the dance floor.

Viktor slid into a space at the crowded bar and began ordering a round of drinks. As he waited, Alexei's eyes were drawn to a group sitting on a mezzanine overlooking the dance floor. The men were dressed expensively – in tailored suits with gold chains draped around their thick necks, and bejewelled watches adorning their wrists – and were accompanied by two blonde women in stiletto heels and micro-dresses. The table was cluttered with glasses and ice buckets chilling bottles of champagne. As one of the women stood up, presumably to go to the toilet, her boyfriend gestured curtly for a subordinate to follow her.

Alexei felt a hand press against his elbow.

'You'd be wise not to stare at those men too closely,' Viktor said softly, presenting him with a beer. 'They're gangsters – not the sort of men who take kindly to being watched.'

'Oh, right,' Alexei said hastily. No matter where he looked, the temperature inside Orbit appeared to be rising. Back at the bar, an overweight American man was sat on one of the stools, surrounded by a coterie of beautiful Russian women. As Alexei watched, one of the women stepped forward and inserted a long, slender leg between his, straddling his thigh before lowering herself carefully into the man's lap. She took the drink from his hand and took a long, meaningful sip from it.

'Looks like that guy's going to have a good night,' Alexei remarked.

'I hope for his sake he can afford it,' replied Viktor. 'Women like that don't come for free. And their pimps aren't known for their easy-going nature.'

The leader of the 88s slipped away across the dancefloor,

replaced by Medved, a bottle of beer in each hand. 'Right,' he growled. 'I'm going to find myself a woman. I'll see you later.' He gave Alexei a warning glance. 'If Svetlana hears one word about tonight, me and you are going to have words. Clear?'

'Crystal,' Alexei replied.

The skinhead grunted, then strode off into the midst of the crowd. Marat hurried after him, pinching a girl's bottom as he negotiated a way past her. She responded with a look of complete disgust that made the teenager snigger. Alexei lingered at the bar, content to take in some of Orbit's dirty glamour. He sipped his drink slowly, watching the men and women slowly circle around one another, marking their targets before going in for the kill.

Eventually Viktor reappeared, this time holding the hand of a young woman in a figure-hugging black dress. He smiled at Alexei.

'You remember Nadia?'

Alexei gaped with surprise. Looking closely, it was indeed Nadia, although this girl in the low-cut dress was a very different creature from the shy student he had met at Moscow State University, or the serious onlooker at the hospital complex.

'Hello, Alexei,' she said, with a flickering smile. She was undeniably beautiful. She was also, Alexei had to remind himself, a member of the violent neo-Nazi gang who had put his girlfriend in a coma – and quite possibly Viktor Orlov's girlfriend. The thought instantly sobered him up.

'Hi, Nadia,' he said cordially.

'I have some business to attend to,' Viktor said, transferring Nadia's hand to Alexei. 'I take it I can trust you to take care of my most precious jewel?'

Viktor gently kissed Nadia's free hand and then walked away. She watched the man leave with something approaching a look of apprehension. They were the strangest couple Alexei had ever met. For the life of him, he couldn't fathom what she saw in Viktor, or how the two of them had even met.

Nadia suddenly stumbled, nearly toppling over on her high heels. Alexei had to reach out and catch her.

'You're drunk!' he said.

'Maybe,' Nadia replied coquettishly. 'Can't a girl have a bit of fun every now and again? Why don't you come and dance with me?'

Alexei allowed himself to be dragged reluctantly on to the dancefloor. As quick and nimble as he could be in the ring, as soon as music started playing he found himself clumsy and leaden-footed. He let Nadia dance around him, the girl giggling as she twirled to the music. Alexei begged her to stop, laughingly pleading dizziness, and they made for a small table in the corner of the club. She sat purposefully in the chair next to him, close enough for her legs to brush against his.

Nadia glanced conspiratorially around the room, then leaned forward and whispered something to Alexei.

'What did you say?' he shouted. 'I can't hear you over the music!'

'You're different!' she said, more loudly this time. 'From the rest of them, I mean.'

'The Eagles?'

'Yes, the Eagles. Who else?' Nadia said bitterly, taking an unsteady sip from her drink. 'I've been around this gang for longer than I can remember. The men – they look the same, they talk the same; they even *smell* the same. But not you, Alexei. You can act the big tough guy all you want, but you can't hide the tenderness inside of you. Not from me. Women can sense these things.'

'What – female intuition?' Alexei scoffed, hopeful that she wouldn't catch the desperate edge to his voice. 'I don't believe in that rubbish. If you knew me better, you wouldn't call me soft.'

Nadia coiled her fingers around his, and drew herself closer. Alexei could feel the swell of her breasts as she pushed herself up against him. 'OK, maybe I get to know you better, then,' she murmured in his ear. 'Leave with me. Right now.'

Alexei swallowed nervously. 'Are you crazy? What about Viktor?'

'Who cares about Viktor?' Nadia replied, making a face. 'I'm not scared of him. Are you? Come back with me, Alexei. I promise you won't regret it.'

Alexei couldn't pretend that there wasn't a part of him that didn't want to leave the club with Nadia. There was a quiet sorrow about her that made him feel protective towards her. But then there was Lena. There was always Lena.

'I'm sorry,' he said finally. 'I can't. You're really sweet but –'

Before he could finish his sentence, Nadia untangled

herself from him and stormed off into the nightclub. Alexei slumped back in his seat with a sigh. He drank by himself for a time, moodily watching other people enjoying themselves. Whereas earlier Orbit had seemed glamorous and exciting, now it just seemed loud and overcrowded. Unable to spot any of the other Eagles among the throng, Alexei pushed his way outside to get some fresh air.

The club's doors were now shut to new entrants, and those who had been queuing in vain for admittance had long since drifted off dispiritedly into the night. The street was cold and still. Alexei checked his watch: 0430. He tried to phone Marat, but there was no response. If the teenager was still inside Orbit, there was no way he would hear it.

Alexei was halfway through a text when a woman's strangled scream rang out. It had come from the alleyway next to the club. Alexei ran over and peered around the corner.

He was shocked to see Nadia lying in a crumpled heap, her dress covered in filth from the alleyway floor and a hunted look in her eyes. Viktor Orlov was standing over her. He was shaking with rage; his calm facade stripped away. As the tattooed Eagle bouncer looked on impassively from the shadows, Viktor picked Nadia up and pushed her up against the wall by her throat. Alexei took an instinctive step forward, then checked himself. His mission would be jeopardized if he got involved – no matter how much he wanted to. Instead he pressed himself against the wall and listened.

'If I want a dumb bitch's opinion I'll find a dog in the street,' Viktor spat.

'Please, Viktor,' sobbed Nadia. 'You're hurting me . . .'

Viktor slammed her against the wall again. 'If I hurt you,' he said through clenched teeth, 'it's for your own good. You need to learn to keep your mouth shut.'

'But you're going to kill her!' Nadia said miserably. 'I know what those emails are about. I know what the package is.'

'You don't know a thing. Not a goddamn *thing*,' Viktor snarled. 'Remember that whatever happens to Petrova can just as easily happen to you. I'll do it myself if necessary. Do you understand me?'

Choked, Nadia nodded quickly. Finally Viktor relented, lowering her to the ground. 'There, there,' he said softly, placing his arm around the cowering girl. 'It's all right. There, there, little sister.'

With that, several things clicked into place for Alexei. Viktor wasn't Nadia's boyfriend – he was her brother! Suddenly her role in the Moscow Eagles didn't seem quite so surprising after all.

Viktor was now making low murmuring noises in Nadia's ear, trying to calm her down. As the trio left the alleyway and returned inside Orbit, Alexei slipped back into the shadowy recesses of a doorway. He waited outside for twenty minutes, until Marat came reeling out of the club, grumbling about all the stuck-up women that had turned him down. As they headed back to the Eagle's apartment, Alexei barely listened to his complaints: all he could think about was Viktor Orlov, his hand wrapped mercilessly around his sister's throat.

19. The Tsar

The men came for them at dawn.

Alexei was fast asleep on Marat's floor when the front door exploded open. He barely had time to work out where he was before masked men were swarming over him, firm hands pinning him to the carpet. Alexei tried to struggle free, but a swift blow to the side of the head stunned him. He heard Marat cry out in surprise, and then someone rammed a woollen balaclava down over Alexei's head – back-to-front, so he couldn't see through the eyeholes. As his hands were roughly bound together, a hand rummaged through his pockets and pulled out his mobile phone, sending it clattering across the room. Now there was no way he could call Trojan for help.

The men hauled Alexei to his feet, manhandling him out of the apartment and down into the car park, where he was bundled into the back seat of a vehicle. He collided with another body – presumably Marat's – as he was thrown alongside him.

'Move and you're dead,' a voice hissed, and then the car door slammed shut.

Alexei tried to stay calm as the vehicle drove away. The biggest danger was that his cover had been blown – but if that was the case, why had the men kidnapped Marat too? Alexei shifted uncomfortably in his seat, every breath only forcing the balaclava's stale odour further down his throat. As the car mapped out a silent path through unseen streets, Marat whimpered quietly.

Then, without warning, someone ripped off his balaclava. Alexei blinked in the morning sunlight. Looking out through tinted windows, he saw that they were travelling along a broad, tree-lined highway in the middle of the countryside. Moscow's grand sprawl was a distant dream. Viktor Orlov was sitting in the front passenger seat, watching the startled teenagers with undisguised amusement.

'What's going on?' Marat blustered. 'Where are we?'

Viktor smiled. 'We thought the pair of you had earned a little drive. You must forgive our rather elaborate caution. We're going to meet someone who guards his privacy fiercely.'

Pulling out a small knife, Viktor leaned over and cut Alexei and Marat free. 'Besides,' he continued, 'it's always good to test your men's mettle. An Eagle has to be prepared for anything. I was pleased to see that neither of you begged for mercy.'

'Though you may want to mewl a little more quietly next time, Marat,' Pavel said pointedly, from behind the wheel.

Alexei glanced around the car in surprise. 'It's only us four?' he asked. 'Where's Medved?'

'Busy explaining his hangover to Svetlana,' the ex-soldier replied. 'Today is a day for business, not action. Not Medved's speciality.'

'You should be flattered,' added Viktor. 'This is the most exclusive of invitations. Occasionally our rendezvous likes to run his eye over our foot soldiers – make sure that they are up to the task. After your clash with the Uzbeks, we felt you should represent the fresh new wave of the Moscow Eagles.'

'Do not make us regret that decision,' Pavel said ominously.

As the car continued along the highway, Alexei caught a glimpse of a turret poking out from above the treeline. The trees began to thin, and he saw that the highway was lined with houses set back from the road along sweeping driveways. Many ordinary Russians had modest dachas they used as countryside retreats, but these houses were a different world altogether – state-of-the-art mansions with swimming pools, satellite dishes, and garages the size of aircraft hangars. Through gaps in electrified railings, Alexei saw chrome flashes of expensive foreign cars: Ferraris, Porsches, Lamborghinis.

He jumped as a sleek black sports car appeared out of nowhere, its bodywork gleaming in the sunlight as it screamed past them. Before Alexei could blink, it had disappeared over the brow of the hill and out of sight.

'Did you see that?' Marat said excitedly. 'That was a Bugatti Veyron! One of the fastest cars ever made! There's only about 200 in the whole world!'

Alexei shook his head. It was hard to believe that only a couple of hours ago he had been sleeping on the floor of Marat's derelict apartment. They continued along the highway for another ten minutes before Viktor tapped

Pavel on the arm and pointed towards a gated driveway. Two men were standing guard outside, sub-machine-guns slung over their backs. As the car pulled up beside them, one of the guards handed Viktor a portable scanner. The Eagles' leader pressed his thumb down on the pad, and a tiny LED flashed green. The guard nodded at Viktor, and the gate swung open.

Pavel steered the car up the long driveway, past a small wooden banya – a traditional steam bath – and up towards an imposing redbrick house with high gabled windows. Two figures were visible on the veranda in front of the dacha. One was a small, powerful man, with a bristling beard covering his square jaw. He was wearing a pair of jeans and the Russian national football shirt. At the man's side sat a slim, beautiful brunette in a jumper and black leggings, her arm draped through his. A silver samovar and tea set were laid out on the table in front of them.

As Pavel parked the car next to a grey, open-top Porsche Carrera, the man in the football shirt rose to his feet. Viktor got out of the car, hurried up to the veranda and embraced him, before kissing the brunette's elegantly extended hand.

As they followed on behind, Marat nudged Alexei, and nodded at the Porsche. 'Not bad!' he whispered.

Alexei shrugged. He had never been that interested in cars. Then he caught sight of the Carrera's personalized number plate.

It was Tsar.

Alexei looked away, praying that the recognition hadn't shown on his face. The Eagles had led him straight to

Tsar! Could this dacha be the fortress – was Rozalina Petrova held captive somewhere within these walls? Alexei silently cursed the fact that the Eagles had taken his phone, and that he had been blindfolded for most of the journey. Depending on the route they had taken, he could be a hundred miles from Moscow, or ten.

His mind was racing as he walked up to the veranda, where the bearded man was shaking Pavel by the hand. The soldier turned around to the two teenagers.

'Marat, Alexei – this is Mr Lebedev.'

Things were starting to make sense now. Darius Jordan had suggested that Tsar might be someone with money and influence – who fit that bill better than a tycoon? Perhaps the riot at the Construktko plant had been a smoke-screen. One thing was for sure – Boris Lebedev didn't look like he was holding any grudges now.

The tycoon sized up Alexei and Marat with a single glance, then nodded with apparent satisfaction. He leaned down and kissed the brunette woman on the cheek. 'Run inside now, little bunny. We have business to discuss that you will only find boring.'

The brunette rose gracefully from her chair and sashayed barefoot inside the dacha, a diamond-studded chain sparkling on her bare ankle. Viktor watched her leave with open admiration.

'Pretty girl,' he said.

'Lilya is a former gymnast,' replied Lebedev. 'An expensive gift I bought myself.' He looked reflective. 'If I had known quite how expensive, perhaps I might have reconsidered.'

'I'm sure she's worth every rouble,' said Viktor.

The tycoon made a dismissive gesture with his hand. 'Save the silver tongue for young girls and vain men,' he said sharply. 'Let's get down to business. I take it your boys can keep their mouths shut?'

'That won't be a problem,' Pavel replied laconically.

Lebedev pointed at the door. 'Then come inside,' he said.

The tycoon led them on a lengthy tour of his dacha, a seemingly endless maze of corridors and rooms; through an opulent dining-room, where a long mahogany table stretched out beneath a row of chandeliers; a conference room, complete with leather swivel chairs and banks of television screens; and an indoor swimming pool, a mosaic of a mermaid on its tiled floor visible through the still blue water. Priceless oil paintings seemed to hang on every wall. But – much to Alexei's disappointment – of Rozalina Petrova, there was no sign.

Upstairs, the bedrooms were expensive hymns to tastelessness: four-poster beds covered with pink and cream drapes and teddy bears. Looking at the burly figure of Boris Lebedev, Alexei guessed that Lilya had been left in charge of the decorating in these rooms.

As they headed down a flight of backstairs to the ground floor, Alexei noticed a further set of dingy steps leading on to a basement door.

'What's down there?' he asked innocently.

Lebedev stopped in his tracks. He turned round slowly and eyed Alexei with contempt.

'It's a cellar,' he said. 'What do you think is down there?

Wine bottles and rats. If you'd like to spend some time down there I'm sure that could be arranged.'

'That won't be necessary,' Viktor said smoothly, as Pavel shot Alexei a vicious look. 'Please forgive Alexei's interruption. He suffers from an excess of enthusiasm.'

Lebedev grunted, unconvinced, then continued on his tour. He didn't brighten up until he entered the games room, a luxurious hideaway boasting two American pool tables and a row of arcade machines. The only things framed on the walls in this room were football shirts, signed by players from some of the biggest teams in the world: Real Madrid, Manchester United, AC Milan.

'Now you see my real pride and joy,' Lebedev said, outstretching his arms. He turned to the two teenagers. 'Now I have matters to discuss with Viktor and Pavel. You can wait for us here. Tonight you will all stay. There is more than enough room.'

Viktor inclined his head. 'You are too kind, Boris.'

'So many people have told me,' the tycoon replied, without any visible pleasure.

As Marat eagerly racked up the pool balls, Alexei watched through a gap in the door as the men filed into the conference room.

'I don't get it,' he said. 'The Eagles trashed Lebedev's place a while back, didn't they? So why's he so friendly?'

'Search me,' said Marat. 'If we need to know then Viktor will tell us. Haven't you asked enough stupid questions already today? Now are you going to break or not?'

Keen not to arouse further suspicion, Alexei picked

up a cue and broke. But throughout the afternoon – as he lost game after game to Marat, much to the boy's evident satisfaction – Alexei couldn't get the thought of the cellar door out of his mind, nor what might lie behind it.

The men didn't emerge until the early evening; Viktor, Alexei noted, looked particularly pleased with himself. Dinner was an awkward affair. Boris Lebedev sat at the head of the dinner table, regaling everyone with stories as he drained glass after glass of champagne. Lilya was nowhere to be seen. Viktor and Pavel listened attentively to the stories – as usual, the former's champagne glass lay untouched in front of him. Further down the table, Marat looked uncomfortable as he wrestled with his oysters, while Alexei thought Lebedev was nothing more than a boor. As the tycoon got more and more drunk, his stories got more repetitive and self-aggrandizing, until even Viktor was struggling to show amusement.

It was a relief when the meal finally ended and Alexei could head up to the room he was sharing with Marat. After his late night at Orbit and the long day at the dacha, Alexei was shattered, but he forced himself to stay awake until Marat's breathing had become deep and regular. Pulling back the covers of his bed, Alexei crept soundlessly from the room.

The dacha was drenched in a pregnant quiet. Alexei sneaked along the hallway past Boris Lebedev's room – where the sound of thick snoring was emanating through the door – and headed down the staircase, wincing with every creaking floorboard. He prowled through the ground floor, barely breathing, until he reached the cellar at the rear of the building.

To his surprise, the door swung open at the faintest touch. As his eyes adjusted to the darkness, Alexei could make out the contours of a series of wine racks. Inching deeper into the cellar, he brushed a cobweb out of his face. A drip was splashing down from the ceiling somewhere.

Behind him, there was the faintest squeak of a door hinge.

'Who's there?'

There was a blur of movement in the shadows. A strong hand wrenched his head back by the hair, and Alexei felt a blade press against his throat.

20. Hot Water

'What the hell are you doing down here?' snarled Pavel. Alexei cried out as the Eagle yanked his head back further, the edge of the knife poised a millimetre from his throat.

'Nothing!' exclaimed Alexei, through clenched teeth. 'I was thirsty so I got up to get a drink from the kitchen. I thought I heard someone down here, so I came down to check.'

'Check for what?' Pavel shouted, pressing his blade against Alexei's skin until it dug into his Adam's apple. 'Lebedev told you there was nothing down here!'

'I know he did. But I did hear something, Pavel, I swear!'

If either of them slipped, Alexei knew that his throat would be sliced clean open. He stood there, eyes closed, for what felt like an eternity. Then he felt the grip on his hair relax, and the knife withdraw. With a gulp, he looked at Pavel, who was tucking his blade back into a sheath on his belt.

'Be grateful it was me who caught you,' the man said grimly. 'If it had been one of Lebedev's men you'd be dead for sure – Eagle or not. This is a dangerous place to go snooping around.'

'I wasn't snooping, Pavel! Honest!'

'It looks like I believe you. But no more night-time wandering, you understand me?' He cuffed Alexei across the back of his head. 'I don't care if you need a piss – do it in your bed.'

'I'm sorry,' Alexei said mournfully.

Pavel shook his head. 'I thought there was a chance Marat might do something brainless, but not you. Get out of here.'

Alexei stumbled away up the cellar steps, rubbing his throat.

Back in his bedroom, as Marat snored softly, Alexei tossed and turned in his bed, unable to shake the feeling of the knife at his skin. Just as he was finally drifting off to sleep, the sound of tyres crunching softly across gravel floated up to his window. Alexei crept to the window and peered outside.

A black limousine was creeping around the front of the dacha, as dark and stealthy as a panther. As it slowed halfway down the driveway, the door to the banya opened and two men hurried out, carrying a slumped woman in their arms. It was Rozalina Petrova. Of course, thought Alexei, kicking himself: Lebedev hadn't taken them anywhere near the steam house! It would have been the perfect place to hide the lawyer. She didn't struggle as the limousine's boot clicked open and the men placed her roughly inside. They closed the boot and jumped into the back of the car, which purred away down the drive-way.

As the vehicle disappeared into the night, Alexei

wondered whether that was the last time he'd see Rozalina Petrova alive.

The next morning, the Eagles ate breakfast in the conference room, slurping coffee and munching on ham and eggs. Alexei studiously kept his head down, his eyes drawn to an architectural model of a skyscraper that formed the centrepiece of the table. 'Moskva Heights' – the tag read – 'Moscow's gateway to the future'. Although Pavel refused to catch Alexei's eye, the boy took heart from the fact that Viktor Orlov seemed to be in a good mood, humming softly to himself as he cleared his plate and wiped his mouth with a napkin.

As the gang began trooping back to their car, Lebedev and Lilya followed them out on to the veranda. The former gymnast was clad in a thick coat of pure white fur that must have cost a small fortune. Boredom was plastered across her face.

'Thanks again for the hospitality,' Viktor said to Lebedev. 'It's a truly amazing residence.'

The tycoon shrugged. 'It's more Lilya's place than mine. I rarely see outside of Moskva Heights these days. Don't contact me until our most pressing business is completed.'

With that, he turned on his heel and strode back inside, without bothering to say goodbye.

For the journey back to Moscow, Alexei and Marat were ordered to put the balaclavas back over their heads, although thankfully this time their hands weren't bound. Neither Viktor nor Pavel spoke, leaving Marat to prattle away in the back seat, apparently unconcerned whether anyone was listening or not.

After only a couple of hours' sleep, Alexei should have been dead on his feet, but his mind was alive with questions. Where had they taken Rozalina Petrova now? Did the fact that they had moved her in the middle of the night have anything to do with Alexei – had Pavel not believed his story after all?

He hadn't reached any conclusions by the time they had returned to Moscow, when he removed his balaclava to be greeted by the familiar sight of the gym off Komsomolskaya Square. The building was empty save for Medved and Svetlana, who were cuddling up to one another on one of the weights benches. Embarrassed, the giant skinhead hastily clambered to his feet as the other gang members entered.

'How did it go?' he asked.

'Not bad at all,' Viktor replied mildly. 'Our sponsor is pleased with the way things are going. If things go to plan, the next few months could be very interesting indeed. It's a great time to be an Eagle, Medved. Now, if you'll excuse us, Pavel and I have some things to discuss.'

'No one go anywhere,' rapped Pavel.

The two men disappeared inside the small office adjoining the gym and closed the door. Alexei grimaced with frustration. He was desperate to get back to the monastery in Taganka to talk to Trojan, but the tone of Pavel's voice had brooked no argument. In an effort to occupy himself, Alexei began peppering a punchbag with blows. Marat lay down on one of the benches and dozed off, while Medved and Svetlana huddled back together.

Eventually the door to the office opened, and Pavel strode out. He beckoned everyone over.

'What is it?' rumbled Medved.

'Something's come up,' Pavel replied. 'We've just received word from our good friends at Storm Hammer.'

Marat pulled a face. 'Those cocksuckers? What do they want?'

'Wait,' said Alexei. 'Who the hell are Storm Hammer?'

'Another White Power gang,' Pavel explained. 'They used to claim that they were the toughest skinheads in Moscow, until we stepped in and showed them otherwise. There's been silence between us ever since. But now that Nikolai is in jail, it seems that they wish to talk with us. Maybe they want to bury the hatchet. Maybe they want to start another war. Either way, we need someone to meet with them.'

'I'll go,' Medved said immediately.

Pavel shook his head. 'No, you won't.' He turned to Alexei. 'You will.'

'What?' screeched Svetlana.

'Look, if Medved wants to go –' Alexei began.

'What Medved wants is immaterial,' Pavel said sharply. 'This is Viktor's organization, and he's decided that you're going.'

'This is bullshit!' spat Svetlana, looping her arm around her bristling boyfriend. 'My baby has been with you since day one. No one's been braver. No one's fought harder. This asshole Alexei's only been here five minutes, and you're letting him take over!'

'Enough, Svetlana!' Pavel roared.

Medved stepped forward and squared up to the ex-soldier. Even though Pavel was nearly a head shorter than the burly skinhead, he gazed up at him without fear. The two men eyeballed each other for several taut seconds, then Medved spat on the floor and stalked out of the gym, with Svetlana trotting after him. Pavel didn't bother to watch them leave.

'Am I going to have a problem with you too?' he challenged Alexei.

The boy shook his head.

'Good.' Pavel handed him a scrap of paper with an address on it. 'Go to the bathhouse here. It's run by men we know – there'll be no one to listen in. Find out what Storm Hammer want, and then report back to me immediately.'

As the soldier marched back into the office, Alexei looked down at the address, frowning.

'A bathhouse?' he said to Marat. 'Seems a funny place to meet another gang.'

'Not really,' the other boy replied. 'That's where all the serious meetings take place. After all,' he added grimly, 'it's harder to hide a weapon when you're naked.'

Tucked away down a quiet side street, the bathhouse was so unobtrusive that Alexei walked past it twice without realizing. It was hidden behind heavily shuttered windows within an old terraced house. Only a tiny brass plaque by the front door gave any hint as to the building's purpose. Alexei hesitantly pushed open the door and walked inside.

He was surprised to find himself in a plush entrance hall, with high ceilings covered in ornate marble decorations. Elegant statues and giant ferns in terracotta pots were dotted around the lobby. Alexei's footsteps echoed on the tiles as he walked towards the counter, where a skinhead was watching a boxing match on a portable television screen. He looked up as Alexei approached.

'You one of Pavel's men?'

Alexei nodded.

'Get changed and go through to the sauna,' the skinhead said. 'I'll send through Storm Hammer when they arrive.'

Alexei walked through into the changing rooms, where he took off his clothes and wrapped a towel around his waist. Painfully self-conscious of the black swastika tattooed on his chest, he was relieved that there was no one there to see him. He packed his clothes away into a locker, and placed the key chain around his neck.

As Alexei wandered through the bathhouse, past an opulent bar and lounge area, and then a large plunge pool, the complete absence of people gave the bathhouse a ghostly atmosphere. He was relieved when he finally found the sauna: a small, wooden-panelled room with benches arranged in a square around a stove stocked with steaming coals. A bundle of branches was propped up against one wall next to a bucket of water. The air was thick with heat.

Alexei settled down on a bench to wait, his skin already glistening with sweat. As doubt gnawed away at his mind, he steeled himself with old memories of

Lena: her burrowing next to him on the sofa on snowy winter nights, the television flickering away in the background; joining him for dinner at Stepan's apartment, giggling at his uncle's dreadful jokes; watching Alexei fight from the back of sports halls and gym, pensively biting her lip but never flinching as the punches rained down upon him. At every turn, Lena had been there for Alexei. He owed it to her not to let her down now.

Alexei was beginning to think he had been stood up when the door to the sauna opened and two men walked in. They were older than Alexei; broad-shouldered men with shaven heads, one with a badly scarred face. They were also fully dressed.

A prickle of apprehension ran down Alexei's spine.

'You Alexei?' the scarred man asked roughly.

'Yeah,' Alexei replied, trying to keep the fear out of his voice. 'You from Storm Hammer?'

The man snorted derisively. 'Storm Hammer? Never heard of them.'

'Then there must have been some kind of mistake,' Alexei said urgently. 'Pavel sent me here to talk to Storm Hammer!'

'There's been no mistake,' the scarred man replied, cracking his knuckles threateningly. 'Pavel didn't send you here to talk. He sent you here to die.'

21. Flesh Wounds

Alexei backed away against the sauna wall.

'Wait!' he said, holding out his palms in a pacifying gesture. 'You don't want to do this!'

The scarred man cocked his head. 'Don't we? The word is that you're some kind of grass. Killing you is going to be a pleasure.'

Alexei frantically weighed up his surroundings. There wasn't enough room in the cramped sauna for evasion – he was going to have to take the men head on, whether he liked it or not.

As his assailants advanced upon him, Alexei picked up the wooden bucket filled with water and tossed it on to the stove, sending a cloud of hot vapour into the air. Caught too close to the blast of heat, one of the men cried out and clutched at his face; Alexei followed up like a cobra, cracking the assailant in the side of his head with the bucket. The man fell to the floor, poleaxed.

His scarred accomplice inclined his head. 'Not bad,' he said admiringly. Opening up his jacket, he slowly pulled a knife from his belt. 'But I'd rather a blade than a bucket.'

They began a macabre dance, Alexei jockeying around

the stove as he strove to keep his attacker at arms' reach. The scarred man was artfully quick, and pretty soon Alexei's hands were covered in defensive wounds, blood mingling with the sweat on his palms. Grinning wolfishly, the man darted in and sliced a painful cut across Alexei's chest. He wasn't rushing to finish him off. He was having too much fun.

As his assailant lunged towards him again, Alexei waited until the last second and then sidestepped the attack, grabbing the man's wrist and clamping it against the burning stove. The scarred man bellowed in pain, dropping the knife to the ground with a clatter. Alexei drove a knee into his gut – only for the man to break free of his grip and direct a headbutt into his face, sending Alexei stumbling back over a bench. Tears springing into his eyes, Alexei staggered to his feet to find the other man waiting for him, gingerly holding his scalded right hand.

'Now you've made me angry,' he rasped.

With a roar, Alexei dropped his head and charged forward, hitting the man squarely in the midriff. He drove forward, his legs pumping, sending the two of them crashing out through the sauna door. Alexei was dimly aware of a brighter room, and slick tiles beneath his feet. As he charged blindly onwards, the scarred man punched him repeatedly in the back, desperately trying to bring them to a halt. Then, suddenly, Alexei felt the ground disappear beneath his feet, and the pair of them went tumbling into the plunge pool.

The landing hit Alexei like a punch in the stomach,

ripping the towel from his waist. Disorientated, he flailed underwater, his limbs entangled with the other man. Sheer survival instinct made Alexei claw his way towards fresh air, exploding through the surface of the pool with a gasp. His assailant was a second slow to follow him – seizing his momentary edge, Alexei grabbed the man's head, his fingers searching out the man's right eye and boring into the socket. The man gave out a high-pitched scream, churning the water around them as he writhed in pain.

Finally relenting, Alexei pushed his attacker's head away and began splashing towards the side of the pool. As he reached out imploringly for the side, Alexei felt something fasten on to his left leg. He turned round to see the scarred man gripping his ankle, a manic look in his remaining good eye. Grabbing the side of the pool for leverage, Alexei lifted his right leg out of the water and directed a booming kick directly into the man's jaw. His head snapped back, and he slumped back into the water.

Using every last ounce of strength in his drained muscles, Alexei hauled himself out of the pool. He crawled across the tiles, coughing up water. Blood was running from the knife wound on his chest. The scarred man was floating face-up in the water, unconscious. Even so, there was no time to recover: Alexei wasn't safe yet.

He forced himself to his feet and stumbled, naked, through the bathhouse, staining the tiles with a pinkish mixture of water and blood. The skinhead behind the reception desk shouted something at him as he staggered through the lobby: Alexei ignored him. Hurtling out through the front door, he raced barefoot into the street. Behind him, he heard the bathhouse door crash open again – and looked over his shoulder to see the skinhead chasing after him.

As Alexei reached the end of the side street, a car screeched to a halt in front of him, blocking his path.

'Get in!' a voice urged him. It was Richard Madison. The Englishman leaned across and opened the front passenger door. Alexei dived inside the car, which hurtled away, leaving his pursuer choking on a cloud of exhaust fumes.

'Ow!' Alexei protested, his voice echoing around the draughty monastery.

'Don't be such a baby,' murmured Valerie Singer. 'Do you want these wounds to get infected?'

The Israeli agent had rolled up her sleeves and was now efficiently washing and bandaging the cuts on his hands and chest. To Alexei's immense relief, he had been spared any withering appraisals of his nudity by Richard Madison, who had dug out a pair of combat trousers and a thick woollen sweatshirt before Valerie had appeared. The three of them were the only people in the monastery – the banks of laptops and television monitors hummed away unmanned. Despite the icy wind howling down through the patchwork roof, and the shadows clustering at the edge of the spotlights, after the bathhouse Trojan HQ felt like the safest place in the world.

'Those guys did quite a number on you,' Madison remarked. 'It's a good job ladies like a scar on a bloke.'

Alexei winced as Valerie cleaned out the deep cut on his chest. 'It would have got a lot worse if you hadn't shown up. How the hell did you know I was there?'

'Valerie organized a seance,' Madison replied, deadpan. 'The ghost of Rasputin pointed us in the right direction.' He laughed. 'How do you think we knew? You haven't been out of our sight, you bloody fool!'

Alexei stared at him incredulously. 'I thought you lost me when they took us from Marat's apartment! You followed us to the dacha? Then you know about Boris Lebedev? He's the guy who's really in charge – he's the Tsar!'

The Englishman nodded. 'That much we managed to piece together. I must admit, I was a bit worried when you and that other lad were marched out of his apartment. Of course Valerie stopped me from interfering. And of course she was right.'

'I always am,' Valerie retorted. 'If we'd have stepped in then, your mission would have been over, and none of us would have known about Boris Lebedev.'

'Touché,' said Madison. He grinned at Alexei. 'However, when you legged it out of that sauna with your bollocks flapping in the wind, something told me it was time to intervene.'

'Wait a minute . . .' Alexei said slowly. 'If you know about the dacha, you must have seen where they took Rozalina Petrova! They took her away in the middle of the night!'

Madison and Valerie exchanged glances with one another.

'We saw the car leave,' the Israeli woman began, 'and tracked its progress on satellite.'

'Where did it go?' Alexei asked, his voice rising with excitement.

'We don't know. Our feed went down. By the time we'd got pictures again, the car had gone.'

'You've got to be kidding me!'

'Even Trojan's resources have limits, Alexei.' Madison swept an arm around the dilapidated monastery. 'Look around you. We do the best we can in the circumstances, but there are always going to be things happening outside of our control. Unfortunately, this happened to be one of them.'

'Great,' Alexei said bitterly. 'All this has been for nothing, then.'

'I wouldn't say that,' a loud American voice intoned. Darius Jordan came striding through the monastery, a sheaf of papers in his hand. 'Thanks to your little trip to the countryside yesterday, I've been able to find out a bit more about Mr Boris Lebedev.'

Madison frowned. 'I still can't work out why he's risking associating himself with the Eagles. Compared to this guy, Viktor and Pavel are small-time.'

'Allow me to clear that up for you. I've spoken to one of our contacts at the Russian Parliament. It seems as though billions of roubles aren't enough for Mr Lebedev – he wants power of a different sort. Word is that he's begun filing registration papers for his own far-right political party. Which he, of course, will lead.'

'What's that got to do with Viktor?'

'If you ask me, Lebedev views the Moscow Eagles as his private street army. He gets the 88s to stir up trouble on the streets; people get scared; issues like immigration and order become national concerns. That creates the perfect conditions for a far-right politician to increase their vote.'

'If you think that sounds far-fetched,' Valerie added, 'it's worked before. Hitler's SA – the Brownshirts – did a similar job for him in Germany during the 1920s and 1930s.'

'And by organizing this fight with the Eagles at his plant,' Alexei said slowly, 'he's got the perfect alibi if anyone tries to accuse him of being involved with them.'

Jordan nodded. 'That seems to be the gist of it.'

'There's got to be some way we can stop him!'

'Nothing easy. We've got no conclusive evidence of his involvement with the gang, and given his level of contacts we'd need to present a cast-iron case for the authorities to take it seriously. At any rate, Lebedev isn't our most pressing concern. Tomorrow the deadline for Rozalina expires. I'm sorry to say that we've got no idea where she's being held now – or any leads. The Moscow Eagles have gone underground. The gym's shut and they're not at any of their other usual haunts.'

'So that's it?' Alexei said glumly. 'We're giving up?'

'Maybe,' replied Jordan carefully. 'Maybe not. There's one possible tactic left we could try. It's a Hail Mary play, and a potentially dangerous one at that, but both our time and our options are limited.'

Richard Madison leaned forward. 'It's up to you, Alexei.

We know what you've gone through to try and break the Eagles – you're going to have the scars to prove it. Believe me, no one's going to judge you if you walk away. But what do you say? Do you want to give this one last shot?'

A kaleidoscope of images from the last few days flickered through Alexei's mind. He had brawled in the street, been ambushed in a bathhouse, and been set on fire. He had narrowly avoided being chopped into pieces in a meat-processing factory. He had spent a week in almost constant danger. And at every turn, behind almost every move, he saw the malevolent hands of Viktor Orlov and Boris Lebedev pulling the strings. Alexei imagined the gleeful look on their faces if their plans succeeded.

'Try and stop me,' he said grimly.

22. Risky Business

Situated by the bend of the Moscow River towards the north-east of the city, Moskva-City was a sprawling, unfinished promise. A brilliant forest of skyscrapers and half-constructed steel towers, the business centre was rising towards the sky pane by pane, rivet by rivet. Cranes swung lazily from side to side, their easy movements disguising their vast loads. Banks of windows gleamed in the crisp spring sunshine.

Even in this landscape of monstrous glass edifices, one structure on the quayside towered above the rest: Moskva Heights. Alexei shielded his eyes from the sunlight as he peered up to the summit of the central tower. Beside him, Richard Madison let out a low whistle.

'Not a bad gaff, even for a billionaire,' he said. 'You certain it's Lebedev?'

Alexei nodded. 'He's got a model of it in his dacha. Says he spends most of his time there.'

'Wish we had more time to reconnoitre the place,' said Madison, with a grimace. 'I don't like sending you up there without knowing exactly what's inside. Especially seeing as you're going in on your own.'

'You could come with me, but I reckon it's going to

be hard enough getting in as it is. Do you really think no one's going to have told Lebedev about me?'

'I'd lay money on it, Alexei, and I'm not a gambling man. Listen, without Lebedev's backing the Eagles are just another street gang, right? They need to show they can carry off the big stuff if he's going to trust them. What do you think old Boris is going to say if Viktor rings him up – a day before Rozalina Petrova is supposed to be killed, remember – and tells him that they think they've got a spy in the ranks? Not only that, but they've tried and failed to kill him. Why do you think Pavel didn't slit your throat in the cellar? Why did he wait until he could get hired hands to do his dirty work for him somewhere quiet and out of the way?'

'Because he didn't want Lebedev to find out?'

'Exactly.' Madison's expression grew serious. 'That doesn't mean he's not a dangerous man, though. Just because Lebedev doesn't fight on the streets like Pavel or Medved, he's still capable of causing great harm. Don't take any more risks than you have to.'

Alexei shook his head. 'You're telling me that *now*?'

'Better late than never, eh?' Madison reached inside his coat pocket. 'Before you go – I've got another present for you.'

Alexei looked down in surprise as the Englishman pressed his mobile phone into his hand.

'How did you get this?' he exclaimed. 'I thought I'd left it at Marat's!'

'You did,' grinned Madison. 'While you two were away in the countryside I had a sneak around your pal's flat.

Recognized your phone and thought you might want it back. It's fair to say that's the only thing of interest I found there. Not exactly the Ritz, that place.'

'You haven't slept there,' Alexei said meaningfully.

Madison patted him on the arm. 'Good luck,' he said. 'I'll be here when you get out.'

The Englishman watched with his arms folded as Alexei crossed the empty plaza towards the skyscraper. With most of the surrounding buildings still to be completed, this part of the business centre was eerily quiet. Alexei hurried over to the revolving door at Moskva Heights' entrance, took a deep breath, then pushed his way inside.

He walked through a sparse lobby completely devoid of decoration, its walls painted a neutral cream colour. No signs or logos gave any clue as to the business that was conducted here. The only person visible was a receptionist sitting behind a high counter, typing at a computer as she talked into a headset. She rang off at the sight of Alexei, her lip curling with disdain.

'Can I help you?'

'I've got a message for Boris Lebedev,' he replied, leaning on the counter.

'Mr Lebedev isn't here,' she said curtly. 'And I doubt he's interested in anything you've got to say. Please leave immediately.'

From nowhere, a hulking man in a suit appeared at Alexei's side, and placed a firm hand on his shoulder.

'He's in, all right,' countered Alexei, 'and believe me, he's going to be *very* interested in what I've got to say.'

His voice dropped to a whisper. 'Tell him I'm from Darknet Security.'

The receptionist paused, and then gestured at the bodyguard to step back. She tapped a number into the phone on her desk, and spoke quietly into her headset. Reluctantly, she looked over to the man in the suit and nodded.

'Take him upstairs,' she said.

The bodyguard placed a hand in the small of Alexei's back and propelled him towards a hallway hosting a row of lifts. Two more men were standing guard either side of a lift at the end of the corridor, the outline of short-barrelled machine pistols clearly visible in shoulder slings beneath their jackets. At a sign from the bodyguard at Alexei's side, one of them pressed a button, and the steel door opened. All four of them squeezed inside. There were no buttons inside the lift: clearly, it only travelled to one destination.

Sandwiched between the three hulking bodyguards, Alexei had barely enough room to breathe. He stared at the floor counter display as it ticked endlessly upwards, willing it to stop. Finally, on floor 46, the lift beeped and the doors opened.

They walked out into a small holding room surrounded by Perspex walls. One of the men pressed his palm against a reader, and the facing wall slid to one side. He gestured for Alexei to enter.

'We'll be watching you,' he growled.

Alexei walked into a vast, open-plan space with floor-to-ceiling windows that drenched the room in sunlight. The office had been decorated with the same lack of restraint as Lebedev's dacha: animal-skin rugs covered the thick white carpet, and precious vases balanced on slender wooden tables. Behind a marbled desk at the far end of the office, a row of television screens displayed a continuous reel of stock-market prices.

Lilya was lounging on a plush leather sofa by one of the windows, her long limbs stretched out across the cushions. A flat-screen television flickered from one brightly lit video to another as she flicked idly through music channels. She didn't bother to look at Alexei as he entered the room.

Boris Lebedev was standing in front of his desk, the tycoon's burly frame covered in a black suit and a white shirt with its top button undone. There was a look of thunder on his face. He gestured curtly at the bodyguards.

'Wait in the foyer. I'll take it from here.'

Lebedev waited until his men had lumbered back outside, then rounded angrily on Alexei.

'What the hell are you doing here?' he shouted. 'I told Viktor not to contact me until our business had been completed. And now you waltz up to my office like it's some kind of Nazi beer cellar!'

Alexei shrugged. He was too tired, and had been through too much, to be intimidated any more.

'Viktor sent me to pass on an urgent message. It couldn't wait.'

'So why didn't he contact me over the darknet?'

'That's the point,' Alexei replied calmly. 'He's not sure how secure it is any more. His sister got cold feet about how you were going to dispose of the package. Viktor wanted you to know in case you ended up saying something you shouldn't on the email.'

Lebedev thumped his fist down on the desk.

'Amateurs!' he seethed. 'He can't even trust his own *sister*?'

'A guy once told me there's just some things you can't control,' Alexei replied implacably. 'Guess family's one of them.'

The tycoon lunged towards him, grabbing Alexei by the neck. He dragged him powerfully over to the window, squashing his face against the glass.

'You see that city, smartass?' he hissed, pointing to the jumbled Moscow skyline. 'It's growing as we speak. Built by my plans, with my bricks and mortar, by my labourers. That's *my* city you're looking at. And I will run it. By the end of the year, my party will be the most influential in the city. I will not let you and your imbecile street thugs ruin my plans.'

He pulled Alexei away from the window and shoved him in the direction of the door.

'Go back to Viktor, and give him this message from me: if he can't trust his sister, then he should do something to nullify her as a threat. I would consider that a sign that my faith in him has not been misplaced. Do you understand my meaning, or do I have to spell it out to you?'

'Oh, I understand all right,' Alexei said gravely.

'Then get the hell out of here.'

Lebedev turned his back on Alexei and fixed his attention

on the TV screens. Inwardly seething, Alexei walked over to the sofa and picked up Lilya's hand. She looked up at him, startled, as if seeing him for the first time.

'It was a pleasure to see you again, Lilya,' Alexei whispered into her ear. He fingered the diamond-encrusted watch on her wrist. 'This is almost as beautiful as you are. Almost.'

The woman rewarded him with a dazzling smile. 'Very kind of you to say so,' she murmured.

'Guards!' roared Lebedev. The men came rumbling back into the office and yanked Alexei away from Lilya.

'Throw this little shit out through the back entrance,' spat the tycoon. 'And don't be too gentle about it.'

As the men fell upon Alexei and manhandled him back into the lift, Boris Lebedev paced up and down his office, muttering darkly to himself. Lilya sighed and returned to flicking through the music channels, unaware of the miniaturized electronic bug now silently recording on the back of her watchstrap.

23. Hate Mail

The bodyguards followed Lebedev's instructions to the letter, hauling Alexei out of the lift and throwing him out through the emergency exit on the ground floor, sending him sprawling to the concrete.

'Come back here again and you're dead,' one of them snarled. Adjusting their suits, the bodyguards stomped back inside the skyscraper and slammed the door shut behind them.

Alexei gingerly picked himself up off the concrete and jogged back through Moskva-City. Richard Madison was leaning against a set of railings by his black people carrier, a pensive expression on his face.

'You OK?' he asked, as Alexei approached.

'Lebedev's goons showed me the quick way out of the building,' Alexei replied ruefully. 'Could have been worse, I guess – at least they didn't set me on fire.'

'It's all relative, I suppose. Did you manage to plant the bug?'

'Think so. Won't know if it's working until we try it. You said I can call it from my mobile?'

Madison nodded, and unlocked the people carrier with his beeper. 'Better off out of sight. Get in.'

They clambered inside the vehicle, where Alexei put his mobile on speakerphone and dialled the number Madison gave him. There was no ring tone, only a click and then a loud rustling sound filled the car. In the background, Alexei heard something smashing – one of Lebedev's expensive vases, he guessed.

'Calm down, baby!' a woman's voice pleaded, over more rustling. 'You're scaring me!'

Madison's brow wrinkled. 'That rustling sounds like clothes. Where did you put the bug?'

'On Lebedev's girlfriend's watch.'

'Right in front of him?' The Englishman laughed in amazement. 'Jesus, you've got some balls!'

Alexei shrugged. 'I figured she wouldn't be on her guard. And wherever he goes, she goes.'

'Sound thinking. You're a natural, lad.'

Over the bug, there was a click as someone picked up a telephone receiver, and then stabbed in some numbers on the handset.

'Viktor?' Lebedev barked. 'Yes, I know this is a surprise, shut up and listen to me. One of your little shits has just been in my office . . . How the hell should I know his name? He came to the dacha with you . . . yes, that one.' Lebedev paused. There was an increasingly incredulous silence.

'You think he's a *what*?' roared the tycoon.

'I'd pay money to hear what Viktor's saying right now,' Alexei said gleefully. 'I bet he's shitting himself.'

'Why didn't you tell me this before?' Lebedev raged. There was another brief pause. 'Well it doesn't sound like you're dealing with it, you cretin! He was in my office! . . . I don't know what he wanted, but my men threw him out. Does this mean our usual communication channel is secure? . . . Well at least you haven't managed to bungle that. It looks like I'm going to have to pay closer attention to this matter than I would have wanted. Email me the details for tonight, and contact me when it's done. I don't want to see you or any of your men until then.'

Lebedev slammed down the phone, cursing loudly.

'Bloody idiots!' he shouted. 'They're going to ruin everything!'

There was some more crackling, and then Lilya said in a breathy whisper: 'Why don't you stop work for a while? I know how to help you relax . . .'

Madison reached across and switched off Alexei's phone. 'Bugger,' he muttered. 'Looks like we're going to have to try and hack Lebedev's account to get hold of the location.'

'I don't think that'll work,' Alexei said doubtfully. 'The darknet is almost impossible to hack into, especially in a few hours.'

'Don't be too sure. We've got some of the best computer guys in the business back at Taganka.'

'OK, then,' agreed Alexei, unplugging his phone and opening the car door. 'You go back to the monastery.'

Madison raised an eyebrow. 'And where might you be off to, son?'

'There's someone else who might be able to help.'

'Not sure this is the right time to be dividing our forces. You want me to come with you?'

Alexei shook his head. 'This one I've got to do on my own.'

It was dark by the time Alexei jogged through the square towards Moscow State University. If anything, the monolithic building was even more imposing at night. There seemed to be some kind of party brewing – the entrance to the university was busy with young people carrying bottles of spirits and crates of beer.

Tagging on to the back of a group of drunk students, Alexei slipped into the lobby and hurried up the stairs, desperately trying to remember the route Marat had taken the last time they had been there. From somewhere, he could hear a thumping dance beat echo through the walls, and faint shouts and squeals of delight.

As he hurried along a corridor, he passed a girl sat on a windowsill, cradling a bottle of vodka. She grabbed his arm and thrust the bottle under his nose; Alexei shook himself free and walked away.

'Screw you, then, asshole!' she shouted drunkenly after him.

No matter how hard Alexei tried to recall the way to Nadia's room, it wasn't long before he was hopelessly lost. In desperation, he stopped a group of boys and asked if any of them knew her. One of the teenagers grinned knowingly and directed him up two floors. Alexei bounded up the stairs, relieved when he finally recognized the door at the end of the corridor. He knocked on it quietly.

There was a shuffling sound within, then the door

opened a crack and Nadia cautiously peered outside. Her eyes widened with surprise.

'Alexei!' she gasped. 'What are you doing here? If Viktor finds out he'll kill you!'

'He's tried that once already,' Alexei replied grimly. 'Can I come in?'

Nadia bit her lip, then beckoned him inside. Her room was swathed in shadows, a lone bedside lamp struggling to ward off the darkness. Nadia wrapped her dressing gown tightly around her and sat down on the edge of the bed. Even in the half-light, Alexei could see the bruises on her neck where her brother had choked her.

Catching the line of Alexei's gaze, Nadia's eyes flashed defiantly. 'Viktor says you're a spy. Is that true?'

Alexei took a deep breath, and sat down beside her. It was all or nothing now. 'Yes,' he said finally. 'I'm working for a secret organization that's trying to bring the Eagles down. When Viktor found out I wasn't to be trusted he tried to have me killed.'

'That sounds like him,' Nadia said softly. 'I suppose I should thank you for not lying to me.'

'I'm sorry I had to come here,' Alexei said. 'I know that being here puts you in danger too. But I didn't have any other choice. You're the only person who can help me save Rozalina Petrova.'

She stiffened. 'You know?'

'Everything,' nodded Alexei. 'I know the Eagles kidnapped her. I know she was held at Boris Lebedev's dacha until I spooked them. I know she's going to be killed tonight. The only thing I *don't* know is where they're going to kill her. But you can help me find out.'

'You must think I'm a monster,' Nadia said, her voice trembling. 'Ever since I learned about her kidnap, I've had nightmares about them killing her. But if I help you and Viktor finds out, you don't know what he'll do to me!'

'Listen to me,' Alexei said fiercely, clutching her hand. 'I don't think you're a monster. I saw what happened outside the club. I know Viktor hurts you. I understand why you help him. But this isn't you, Nadia! You're not a Nazi! You're not evil like he is!'

'You understand, Alexei?' Nadia said bitterly. 'You've known Viktor for five minutes; I've spent my life with that bastard. Our parents died when I was a baby – he brought me up. You get used, eventually, to the beatings and the intimidation. I spend time with his subhuman cronies; I upload their sick videos. But you know what the worst thing is, the realization that really breaks you?' She looked down at her hands. '*He's all I've got.*'

Nadia sat motionless as tears fell silently from her eyes.

'Hey,' Alexei said softly, putting his arm around her. 'I can't begin to imagine what you've been through. But if you let Viktor get away with this, then nothing's ever going to change. Help me stop him, Nadia. Don't let this woman die.'

They sat in silence in the shadowy room. Then Nadia wiped the tears away with the back of her hand and briskly stood up. Opening her laptop, she began tapping away on the keys. Within seconds she was logged on to the darknet.

'Viktor protects his email with a password. Luckily for us, he never changes it – and I hacked his account a few months ago.' She pointed at the screen. 'See? He sent Tsar a message an hour ago.'

She clicked on the message, which said only:

2200 hrs. Novodevichy Cemetery.

'They're going to kill her in a graveyard,' Alexei said, suppressing a shiver.

'That sounds like Viktor,' Nadia said darkly. 'He always knew that Rozalina's death would be a more powerful symbol than Borovsky's release could ever hope to be.'

Alexei glanced at his watch. 'I'd better make sure it doesn't happen, then. Haven't got long to get there.'

'You can't go to the cemetery, Alexei!' gasped Nadia. 'It's too dangerous! What about this secret organization of yours; or the police?'

'I can't trust the police. I'll call my company but they're on the other side of Moscow, and we haven't got the time.'

'But they'll kill you!'

'That's a risk I'm going to have to take.' Alexei scribbled down his phone number on a writing pad. 'If you get into trouble, call me. Whatever happens, I'll make sure that Viktor doesn't hurt you. I promise.'

He hugged the girl gently, whispered 'thank you', and turned for the door.

'Wait!' Nadia grasped his arm. 'Before you go, tell me one thing: why are you doing this?'

Alexei hesitated. 'Some of the Eagles beat up my girlfriend, Lena,' he said finally. 'She's still in a coma now. I swore that I'd get revenge – Trojan just came along at the right time.'

'Oh my God.' Nadia's hand flew to her mouth. 'Did it happen on the metro?'

'Yes! Did you hear about it? Do you know who did it?'

Nadia nodded. 'It was Marat and Medved. Marat boasted about it to me. He thought I'd be impressed.'

Alexei felt his stomach tighten with rage. All the time he had been around the Eagles, it had been the people he'd known best who had hurt Lena. They had been within his grasp all along.

'What are you going to do?' asked Nadia.

He looked back at her from the doorway. 'First of all I'm going to find Rozalina. Then I'm going to kill as many of the bastards as I can.'

24. Grave Trouble

The party was spiralling into chaos. As Alexei marched back towards the stairs leading down to the lobby, students were spilling out into the corridor, arms draped around one another as they stumbled back to their dormitories. Music thundered out from one of the rooms, speakers crackling with the sheer volume. Stepping over the prone form of a boy asleep in the middle of the hallway, Alexei got out his mobile and called Trojan. Darius Jordan answered on the second ring.

'We're nowhere here,' he admitted. 'What have you got for me?'

'Novodevichy Cemetery,' replied Alexei. 'Ten o'clock.'

'Well done, son. We're on our way.'

Alexei didn't break stride as two girls stumbled into him, howling with laughter. 'I'll see you there,' he said.

'You've done your part. Leave this to us now.'

'But you won't get there in time!' Alexei protested. 'It's already half past nine, and I'm much closer than you are!'

'Stay away from the cemetery,' Jordan said tersely. 'That's an order. The Eagles will be armed and in numbers. You're not prepared for this.'

'Do what you like. I've been through too much to walk away now.'

'Alexei –'

He flipped his mobile phone shut, cutting off the American in mid-sentence. Alexei took a final look back at the party, then turned his back on it and strode down the stairs. He was halfway across the lobby when he heard a voice calling out his name.

'Wait for me!'

Alexei turned round to see Nadia hurrying through the hall after him. She had changed into a pair of jeans, and was pulling a coat over a thick jumper.

'You'll never get to Novodevichy in time if you take the metro,' she explained, jangling a set of car keys beneath his nose. 'I'll drive you there.'

'Are you sure?'

Nadia nodded. 'You were right. I've let my brother get away with things for far too long. It's time to make a stand.'

Torn, Alexei scratched his cheek. He had placed Nadia in enough danger just talking to her – he didn't want to make the situation worse. But given that he had just ignored Darius Jordan, how could he deny Nadia the right to defy the Eagles as well?

'OK,' he said finally. 'Lead the way.'

She took him outside to a small car park in front of a laboratory, and unlocked a white Lada. Alexei got inside, shivering in the freezing cold air. Nadia flicked on the headlights and drove into the night, the Lada's engines shrieking in protest as she floored the accelerator. Alexei sat in silence, nervous energy surging through his system. This was the calm before the storm – like sitting in the changing room minutes before one of his kickboxing fights. He tried to keep calm, focusing on the impending collision with the Eagles. As the car careered through the streets of Moscow, Alexei saw himself walking slowly towards the ring, bouncing on his toes and banging his gloves together. Whatever happened tonight, someone was going to lose. Alexei just had to make sure that it wasn't him.

Nadia bounced the Lada across an intersection and took a sharp right, on to a road that followed the curve of Moscow River. They hurtled past an imposing turreted building, its golden domes rising up behind a high stone wall.

'That's Novodevichy Convent,' said Nadia. 'The cemetery's right next to it.'

As she spoke, the convent passed out of sight and a long railing appeared in front of a line of trees. Nadia pulled over by the entrance – a heavy metal gate between two squat, red-brick buildings.

Alexei glanced at the high gate in desperation. 'How the hell am I supposed to get inside there?'

The gateway to the cemetery opened, and a security guard appeared in the driveway.

'Leave that to me,' Nadia said. She kissed him fiercely on the lips. 'Good luck,' she whispered, and then she was gone. Alexei watched as she ran up to the guard, catching him before he could lock the cemetery gates.

'Excuse me,' she called out, with a shy smile. 'I'm lost. Could you help me?'

The guard grinned, and pushed his cap back on his head. 'I'll do my best. Can't have a pretty girl like you wandering around on her own at night. Where are you trying to get to?'

Nadia launched into a long and complicated explanation, pointing away down the road so the guard was forced to turn his back on the entrance. Alexei slipped out of the Lada and crept through the shadows towards the gate. He heard Nadia's tinkling laugh, and then he slipped through the open entrance into the graveyard.

Novodevichy Cemetery was enshrouded in a portentous quiet, its graves spread out among towering trees. Following a broad path through the dark, Alexei plunged deeper into the cemetery, past a sombre honour guard of headstones. Some of Russia's most famous artists and statesmen were buried here; every footstep took Alexei past a glorious episode from his country's past. His senses were working on overdrive, alert to every leaf rustling in the wind, and every small animal scuttling through the undergrowth.

As Alexei hurried along the path, he checked the time on his phone. It was ten minutes to ten. He was running out of time – there was too much ground to cover on his own. The cemetery was a vast maze of paths and graves, a labyrinth of the dead. Alexei prayed that Trojan were closing in on the cemetery. How quickly could they get across Moscow?

Just as Alexei was beginning to give up hope, a woman's scream rent the air.

He broke into a flat-out sprint, skirting between graves

as he left the path and hurtled through the trees. He ran towards the sound, willowy branches lashing his skin, his stomach lurching at the thought that he might be too late. An exposed tree root caught his foot, sending him crashing to the ground. Hearing voices ahead, Alexei picked himself up and crept towards them. He crouched down behind a giant birch and peered around its trunk.

He looked out on to a small clearing amid a knot of trees, backed by a row of ivy-tangled tombstones. Rozalina Petrova was on her knees in front of the tombstones, her hands bound behind her back. A gag had fallen from her mouth, and was hanging around her neck. Three men were standing around her: Marat, Medved and Viktor Orlov. The leader of the Moscow Eagles was pointing a pistol at her head.

'If I were you, I wouldn't scream again,' he said matter-of-factly. 'There's more than one way to die – and some of them are infinitely more painful than others. I'm not squeamish.'

Viktor looked as unruffled as ever, his dark suit pressed, his side-parted hair wavering slightly in the wind. Medved looked on impassively at his side, his burly arms folded. A few paces away, Marat's face was pale as he glanced around the clearing, his fingers drumming nervously on the strap of the digital camcorder in his right hand. For all the boy's violent bluster, Alexei doubted whether he had the stomach for murder.

'Isn't it ten o'clock yet?' Marat asked jumpily. 'Let's get this thing over with.'

Viktor shot the boy a murderous glance. 'There's still

ten minutes to go. You just make sure you're ready to film when the execution begins. We want the world to witness our actions. Now is not the time for doubt, Marat. Tonight you're going to prove yourself a true Russian hero.'

Icy rage coursed through Alexei at the man's words. These were the scumbags who had hurt Lena – and now they were going to murder an innocent woman in cold blood. He was shocked to hear the sound of thin laughter carry across the clearing. It had come from Rozalina Petrova.

'A true Russian hero?' she said faintly. 'Does this execution count as an act of heroism?'

'Shut your mouth, bitch,' barked Medved.

Rozalina's eyes blazed with defiance. 'I'm not scared of you,' she said, her voice unwavering. 'Kill me; don't kill me. You're still cowards. No matter how many people you murder, there will always be true Russians lining up to defy you.'

She closed her eyes as Viktor pushed her forehead back with his gun.

'Your death is only the beginning,' he said grandly. 'The Moscow Eagles will soon dominate the streets of this city. And with our backer's support, it will not be long before the state marches in step with us.'

'If you believe that,' Rozalina said through clenched teeth, 'then you're even more stupid than I gave you credit for.'

Viktor slapped her across the face with an open palm, sending her crashing to the grass. Alexei had to grip the birch to stop himself from running to Rozalina's aid. He couldn't believe how brave she was. But the seconds were still ticking away, and Trojan were still nowhere in sight: Alexei was on his own. Outnumbered and out-gunned, it didn't look like there was anything he could do.

Still, thought Alexei as he steeled himself, there was no way that he was leaving Rozalina to face the Eagles alone . . .

He was clambering to his feet when a twig snapped behind him, and a cold gun barrel dug into the back of his head.

'Don't move,' a voice breathed in his ear. It was Pavel.

25. Avenging Angels

'I had a feeling you'd show up,' the ex-soldier said softly. 'Knew you wouldn't be able to resist sticking your nose in. How did you find out we were here?'

'Lucky guess,' Alexei retorted.

Pavel chuckled mirthlessly, then struck Alexei across the back of his head with his handgun. Bright cloudbursts of pain exploded in front of Alexei's eyes as he fell to the ground. Through blurred vision, he saw Viktor Orlov glance over in their direction.

'Who's there?' he snapped.

'It's me,' Pavel called back. 'With an uninvited guest.' Hauling Alexei to his feet, he marched him into the clearing at gunpoint. Viktor's eyes lit up at the sight of them.

'So glad you could join us, Alexei!' he crowed. 'I was most disappointed when you escaped from the little party we'd thrown for you at the bathhouse. May I introduce Rozalina Petrova?'

The lawyer looked up uncomprehendingly at Alexei, her eyes those of startled prey. At the edge of the clearing, Marat turned his back and shifted uncomfortably from foot to foot, unwilling to look at his erstwhile friend. By contrast, Medved was only too keen to press his face up against Alexei's.

'I should have listened to Svetlana,' he growled. 'She knew you were full of shit from day one.'

'Don't let her do all of your thinking,' Alexei replied. 'She's just as stupid as you are.'

Viktor grabbed the skinhead by the shoulder, pulling him away. 'Leave this to me, Medved,' he said calmly. The leader of the 88s inspected Alexei through his horn-rimmed glasses.

'Since you're here,' he said, 'why don't you enlighten us as to the identity of your employers? I presume you're not acting alone. Is it the police? The government? Some other cowardly and treacherous organization that fears the might of the Moscow Eagles?

'Go to hell,' replied Alexei, and spat in Viktor's face.

For a second time, Pavel brought his gun down on the back of Alexei's head – harder this time. Alexei collapsed to the turf beside Rozalina Petrova. There was a roaring sound in his ears. It felt like someone had dropped an anvil on his head.

Viktor pulled a tissue from his pocket and slowly wiped his face clean. 'Now that,' he said softly, 'was a mistake.'

Alexei crawled to his knees, still holding the back of his head. He was going to die in this clearing. He knew it for certain. But although he was scared, there was no way he was giving Viktor the satisfaction of showing it. Not when Rozalina was next to him – kneeling but unbowed.

'I'm not scared of you,' he said, through gritted teeth.

'Oh, but you should be,' Viktor replied.

'He's just a boy!' Rozalina begged. 'Do what you must with me, but don't kill the boy!'

Viktor ignored her, and turned to Pavel. 'Who do you think we should shoot first – the bitch lawyer or the back-stabbing traitor?'

Pavel shrugged. 'As long as they both die I don't care.'

'The efficient attitude of the fighting man,' remarked Viktor, with a smile. He pointed the gun at Alexei. 'The traitor it is.'

Alexei closed his eyes. Images of Lena flashed through his mind. *I never got the chance to say goodbye*, he thought to himself.

There was a loud report in the clearing, and Alexei heard someone cry out. Opening his eyes, he was astonished to discover that he was still alive, and that Viktor was clutching his right arm, his gun lying on the ground.

'Someone's in the trees!' Orlov yelled.

Pavel whirled round, training his handgun on the woods. His heart singing with relief, Alexei made out a shape darting through the darkness: Trojan had arrived.

As bullets zinged through the clearing, the Eagles scattered like ninepins, diving to safety behind the headstones. With a loud oath, Pavel fired off a couple of rounds, then dragged Viktor out of the line of fire.

'Forget about me!' Viktor screamed. 'Kill the lawyer!'

Snarling, Pavel turned round and pointed his gun at Rozalina. Without thinking, Alexei dived headlong, knocking the lawyer to the ground as a bullet whistled through the air where she had been kneeling and bit into the headstone behind her.

'Stop right there!' a female voice commanded in Russian.

Alexei looked across to see that Pavel had frozen in between shots, a wisp of smoke wafting from the barrel of his gun. Behind him, Valerie Singer emerged from the shadows like an apparition, her gun trained on the back of Pavel's head.

'Drop the weapon,' she said crisply, before calling out: 'Madison!'

The Englishman appeared at the edge of the clearing, calmly reloading his weapon. 'Present,' he said.

Gesturing with her gun, Valerie ushered Pavel into the centre of the clearing.

'You too, Orlov,' she said.

Viktor grudgingly obeyed, hate smeared across his face like a bloodstain. He clutched at the wound in his arm.

'That's two of them,' Madison said, scanning the head-stones. 'Where did the other two go?'

A loud crashing sound made them whirl round – Medved broke from his cover, barrelling into the trees. As Alexei watched, Marat peered out from behind another of the gravestones, his face ashen as he weighed up whether to make a run for it. For a brief second, the teenagers' eyes met. Then Marat bolted.

'Stay where you are, Alexei!' Valerie cried out.

But Alexei was already running into the trees. He plunged into the darkness after Marat, darting in and out of the birches, his eyes fixed on the boy's bright red sweatshirt. Behind him, Richard Madison was calling out his name. Alexei redoubled his efforts, closing the gap on Marat as the other boy stumbled in fear. As the cemetery gate appeared on the horizon, Alexei rugby-tackled Marat, sending both of them crashing to the floor.

'No!' Marat cried, as Alexei pinned him down. 'Please!'

'You hurt Lena!' Alexei said, his voice ragged.

'Who?'

'My girlfriend. On the metro. You and Medved.'

Marat's eyes widened with terror. 'Her? I never knew! I'm sorry, Alexei! Please don't hurt me!'

Alexei wasn't thinking clearly any more. The next thing he knew, he had punched Marat hard in the face, and was banging his head against the ground. Marat's nose was twisted and bleeding profusely, and Alexei must have hit him again. Then, dimly, he was aware of a strong hand pulling him off the other boy.

'Enough, Alexei!'

Alexei whirled round, his fists clenched. Richard Madison held his hands up in the air.

'It's only me,' the Englishman said softly. 'We're the good guys. Remember?'

'Yeah,' Alexei said dully, suddenly aware of the damp blood on his knuckles, and Marat's senseless heap on the ground. 'I don't know what happened. I was so angry . . .'

His voice faltered. Madison wrapped an arm around his shoulder. 'It's all right, lad. You've been through a lot. It happens to the best of us.'

'What about Medved? Did you catch him?'

Madison shook his head. 'He managed to give us the slip. But we'll catch up with him. The most important thing is that you and Rozalina are safe, and Viktor is in our hands. If Valerie hasn't already killed him.'

They walked slowly back to the clearing, carrying the slumped form of Marat between them. Valerie was standing guard over Viktor and Pavel, her arm straight and unwavering as she trained her gun on them. Rozalina Petrova stood behind her.

'I suppose you're pleased with yourself, you bitch,' sneered Viktor.

'*Jew* bitch,' Valerie replied coolly. 'And I'd be happier putting a bullet in between your eyes.'

'Do it, then,' said Viktor. 'I'd rather die than submit myself to subhumans.'

Valerie smiled thinly. 'Why do you think you're still alive? You're going to have a long time in prison to live with this indignity.'

'Prison?' Viktor smiled glassily. 'Oh no. I don't think so.'

His hand snaked into his jacket pocket, bringing out a tiny .22 calibre pistol.

'Look out!' Alexei cried.

Valerie didn't even need to shoot. In one movement, Viktor pressed the .22 to his head and fired. The gun's report echoed around the clearing like a death-knell as the leader of the Moscow Eagles dropped to the ground.

In the silence that followed, Pavel glanced down at the .22, lying inches from Viktor's outstretched hand, then back at the gun trained on him.

'Feel free to try for it,' Valerie said icily. The soldier took a final look at the .22, then shook his head.

'Pity,' she murmured.

As Richard Madison handcuffed Pavel and the immobile Marat, Alexei stood stock-still, unable to take his eyes away from Viktor's corpse. A pool of blood was spreading out across the grass from the man's gaping head wound.

He realized that someone was standing at his side. It was Rozalina Petrova. She looked up at Alexei, then dissolved into floods of tears.

'It's OK,' he whispered, gently holding her shaking frame. 'It's over.'

26. Mission End

The monastery echoed to the sound of activity as Trojan Industries closed down their Russian headquarters. Operatives bustled around Alexei, packing up laptops, rolling up electricity cables and unplugging the television screens. The spotlights were switched off and carried away, leaving the hall in dusty darkness.

Alexei was standing in the centre of the hall with Rozalina Petrova, Darius Jordan and Richard Madison. The American's face was wreathed in a smile.

'I'm delighted to say that Trojan's second mission has been as successful as its first,' he proclaimed. 'We've achieved both our primary objective – rescuing Ms Petrova – and our secondary objective – breaking up the command structure of the Moscow Eagles. And all thanks to Alexei. I tell you straight, son: if you ever want a job in the intelligence service, you come and find me.'

Alexei laughed. 'Thanks, but I've been shot at enough to last me a lifetime. I'm looking forward to getting back to normal, boring life.'

'Fair enough.' Jordan turned to the human rights lawyer. 'And what about you, Ms Petrova? After all you've been through, do you think you might take a break for a while?'

'Are you kidding me?' The lawyer's face was pale but determined. 'Pavel and Marat may be in custody but they haven't been convicted yet. I need to make sure they join their friend Borovsky in prison. This is no time to take a break, Mr Jordan. The Moscow Eagles aren't the only skinhead gang in Russia.'

'Too true. At least we've put a stop to the 88s. Medved may have evaded us in the cemetery but the police are combing Moscow for all the members of the Eagles – he can't hide forever. And I'd wager both Pavel and Marat will sing like canaries in the hope of getting a lighter sentence. Which should mean our friend Boris Lebedev will get a knock on his door before too long.'

'That'll put a dent in his political ambitions,' Richard Madison added. 'Difficult to run for office from a prison cell.'

Jordan looked around the monastery, frowning. 'We seem to be missing someone. Where's Valerie?'

'Said she had something to do before we left,' the Englishman replied with a shrug. He grinned at Alexei. 'I wouldn't hold out too much hope of an emotional goodbye, or a parting gift. She's not that kind of woman.'

'When you see her, will you tell her thanks?' Alexei asked. 'She saved my life back in the cemetery – I never got a chance to say that.'

'Count on it,' replied Richard Madison. 'Now, before we go, I believe that Yelena here is going to help you with something.'

The pretty make-up artist stepped forward.

'Ready to start treating that tattoo?' she asked. 'You'll need quite a few sessions under the laser, but I'll be in Moscow for as long as you need. By the end you'll be as good as new.'

Alexei paused. 'When you put the swastika on me, Richard said you're an expert.'

'I know what I'm doing,' she replied modestly.

'Instead of removing the tattoo, can you change it to something else?'

'Of course.' Yelena nodded. 'I only thought you'd want it completely removed.'

'So did I,' said Alexei. 'But I've been through too much to turn my back on it all now it's over. There should be some kind of reminder.'

'It might take a bit of time, but my kit's still here,' Yelena said. 'What did you have in mind?'

Alexei smiled.

By the time Alexei had gingerly pulled his sweatshirt back on, the last of the equipment had been removed from the hall. There was no clue that Trojan had ever been there; not a single footprint in the dust. A wooden beam creaked in the silence.

'Right,' Richard Madison said briskly, clapping his hands together. 'Home time.'

Outside the monastery, a convoy of unmarked vans was crunching away down the driveway. Only the black people carrier remained parked by the entrance. Jordan rubbed his hands together.

'Don't get me wrong, I like Moscow,' he said conversationally. 'But Miami's a damn sight warmer.'

'Stick around for the summer,' Alexei replied. 'You'd be surprised how hot it can get.'

'You know, part of me wouldn't mind doing that – I reckon you could have a lot of fun in this city. But duty calls. Trojan's barely started. There are plenty of other gangs out there just as unpleasant as the Moscow Eagles.'

'Where will you go next?'

'I have absolutely no idea,' Jordan replied, looking over the Moscow skyline. He continued, in a softer voice: 'But even though we're leaving, rest assured that Lena's treatment will be paid for – no matter how long it takes. She'll wake up soon, son.'

'Thanks.'

'Thank *you*, Alexei.'

Stretching out a large hand, Jordan firmly shook Alexei's. The American strode over to the people carrier and climbed inside. Behind Alexei, Richard Madison closed the monastery door and chained it up. He gave Alexei a quick hug, patting him on the back.

'Well done,' he muttered. 'I'm bloody proud of you.'

'Wish my uncle agreed with you,' Alexei replied gloomily.

'Ah. Going off to patch things up with the old man now, eh? He'll come round.' Madison's eyes twinkled mischievously. 'Us military men can be a bit slow on the uptake, but we get there in the end.'

The Englishman nodded at the people carrier. 'Want a lift anywhere?'

Alexei shook his head. 'I need the walk to work out what I'm going to say to Stepan.'

'Fair enough. You take care of yourself.'

Madison hauled himself into the driver's seat, then started up the engine. With a merry beep on its horn, the people carrier rolled away down the winding driveway and out of sight, leaving Alexei alone on the bleak hill.

If anything, Alexei felt even more nervous approaching his uncle's flat than he had done entering Novodevichy Cemetery. No matter how much he rehearsed what he was going to say, nothing sounded right in his head. Even though his mission had ended, Alexei still felt honour bound to keep it a secret. Exposing Trojan Industries to public scrutiny might threaten Lena's care.

He had just turned into Stepan's home street when there was a loud squeal of tyres, and a white car sped away from the entrance of his uncle's apartment block. A sudden fear washing over him, Alexei sprinted down the street and bounded up the stairs to Stepan's apartment. Hammering on the door, he was relieved when it quickly opened, revealing his uncle. Stepan was wearing a white vest and dark-brown trousers, a pair of reading glasses perched on his nose. His face brightened with surprise.

'Alexei!' he cried, enfolding his nephew in a warm bear-hug. 'I'm so pleased to see you again!'

'You are?' Alexei replied, laughing with surprise.

'Of course!' Stepan exclaimed. 'I know I was angry, but it's because I was so worried – and upset you wouldn't tell me what was going on.'

'Before you say anything else, look.' Alexei pulled up his sweatshirt, revealing a fresh tattoo on his chest: a phoenix, soaring up from a bed of flames. The swastika had been completely obscured, erasing the last grubby fingerprints of the Moscow Eagles.

'I got rid of the swastika, like I promised I would,' Alexei said solemnly. 'I'm sorry that I still can't tell you why I had it, though.'

'No need. I've just had a visitor who's explained everything to me.'

Alexei's eyes widened. 'What – *everything*?'

'Well, everything she can. I'm a soldier, Alexei – no one has to tell me the importance of mission secrecy. But I do know that an innocent woman is alive today because of you.' Stepan gave him a sober look and patted him on the cheek. 'I am very proud of you, nephew. And your father would be too, if he knew.'

'You won't tell him, will you?' Alexei asked anxiously. 'If word ever got out, it could spell trouble – not just for me, but Lena too.'

Stepan placed a hand across his heart. 'You have my solemn word. Now come inside! You look like you haven't eaten since I last saw you.'

His uncle ushered him into the lounge, which was thick with smoke. Cigarettes were piled high in the ashtray. Alexei smiled. It appeared that Valerie Singer had given him a parting gift of sorts, after all.

The call came for him in the middle of the night. Immersed in a dark, shapeless dream, it took Alexei several seconds to rouse himself and answer his mobile.

'Hello?' he said drowsily.

'Alexei!' A girl's voice. She was sobbing hysterically. Alexei sat up in bed.

'Nadia? What is it – what's wrong?'

'I'm sorry, Alexei!' she cried. 'I tried not to tell him but he was hurting me . . .'

'Slow down, Nadia!' urged Alexei. 'Who hurt you?'

'Medved,' she said miserably. 'He jumped out at me as I was getting into my room. He said that you'd turned up at the cemetery and ruined everything. He figured out that I must have helped you, and asked me all sorts of questions about you. At first I pretended I didn't know what he was talking about, but then he started getting rough . . .'

'It's OK,' Alexei said soothingly. 'I understand. You did all you could. What exactly did you tell Medved?'

'I told him about Lena. About how he'd hurt her and that she was now in the hospital and that's why you were doing what you were doing.'

A cold shiver of dread ran down Alexei's spine.

'Listen to me, Nadia: where's Medved now?'

'I don't know. As soon as I told him about Lena he stormed out of my room. I think he may have gone after her. Hurry, Alexei!'

He was already halfway through the door.

Alexei didn't remember much of his journey to the hospital. It was a long nightmare of rainy, empty streets. He tried to flag down every car that passed, but no one was willing to pick him up. He ran until his lungs were burning and his legs heavy with tiredness. His face glistened with rain and sweat. With every stride, Alexei was driven on by the thought of Medved, and what he might do to Lena if he was alone with her . . .

Eventually the hospital drew into view. Alexei skirted round a parked ambulance and exploded into the reception.

'Hey!' the nurse cried out as he ran past her desk. 'Where do you think you're going?'

A doctor tried to grab him by the arm – Alexei shoved him off, and bounded up the stairs three at a time. Ignoring the shouts of protest from behind him, he sprinted along the hospital corridor, crashing through the door into Lena's room.

His girlfriend was still lying frozen in the bed, the steady beeping of the heart monitor the only clue to the fact that she was alive. Only now she wasn't alone. There, looming over Lena's bedside, was Medved.

27. Death Match

'Get away from her,' Alexei said, through clenched teeth.

Medved didn't move. He was staring at Lena, a large hand ominously stroking her cheek. The giant skinhead's clothes were torn and stained with mud. Usually a blustering whirlwind of rage, there was an eerie calm about Medved that only deepened Alexei's unease.

'I remember this girl,' Medved rasped. 'She stuck her nose in where it wasn't wanted. Just like you.'

'If you touch a hair on her head,' Alexei began, 'I'll . . .'

The skinhead halted him with a scornful look. 'You'll what? Where are your friends now, Alexei? Where are their guns? It's just you and me. Do you really think you can stop me?'

Alexei stepped forward meaningfully. 'If I have to,' he said. 'But it doesn't have to come to that, Medved. Viktor's dead. Pavel and Marat are in jail. Whatever happens here, the Eagles are finished. Don't make things any worse than they already are.'

Medved shook his head. 'It's not over yet,' he said. 'We're still here.'

'Look, the police are going to be here soon,' Alexei

tried, desperation creeping into his voice. 'If you leave now, maybe you can get away.'

'I don't want to get away,' the skinhead replied, in a far-away voice. When he looked up at Alexei again, his eyes were granite-hard with intent. 'I want everyone to know what I've done.'

As Alexei gazed at Medved, in the stillness of the hospital room he could almost hear the tension crackling between them. Lena's heart monitor continued to mark time – her steady rhythm a sharp contrast to the skittish pounding within Alexei's chest.

'Your quarrel is with me,' Alexei said quietly. 'Leave Lena out of it.'

'Don't tell me what to do.'

Beep, beep, persisted the heart machine. Alexei tensed.

It was almost a relief when it began – Medved rumbling across the hospital room like an avalanche. Alexei slipped into a fighting stance and threw a right cross at the skinhead, but the punch glanced off the side of his head. With a feral roar, Medved enfolded Alexei in a crushing bear-hug and lifted him off the floor. The air rushed from Alexei's lungs as the skinhead's burly arms tightened around his chest. He squirmed as he fought for breath, his arms pinned to his side, his feet dangling helplessly in mid-air. Medved bellowed in triumph, his face flushing with effort.

Alexei's ribs felt like matchsticks in his chest, and he was becoming giddy from the lack of oxygen. As a black tide overwhelmed him, he pulled back his head and drove it into Medved's face. The skinhead yelled with pain, dropping Alexei as he reeled backwards, blood gushing from his nose. Alexei collapsed, his lungs gasping painfully for air. At the back of his mind, he was aware of an alarm bell ringing somewhere in the hospital. Even if help was on its way, he knew that it wouldn't be here quickly enough to save him.

Pinching his bleeding nose, Medved stumbled back over to Alexei and kicked him viciously in the side. Alexei cried out, crumpling like an empty crisp packet. He curled up into a ball, hands over his head, as the skinhead rained blows upon him. In desperation, Alexei lashed out a leg, catching Medved in the gut and knocking him backwards.

It was only a temporary reprieve; Medved came mercilessly back at him, holding Alexei down with one hand as the other thundered into his face again and again. Numb with adrenaline, Alexei didn't feel pain, only a sense of overwhelming helplessness as the skinhead's fist rose and fell.

And then the blows stopped. Alexei felt the skinhead release him, heard his slow, deliberate footsteps as he moved to Lena's bedside. Alexei groaned, his mouth thick with the taste of blood. Medved snorted.

'Your girlfriend put up more of a fight than you did,' he said dismissively. 'Stay there if you want, while I mess up her pretty face some more.'

Spluttering blood, Alexei rolled on to his front and began clawing hand-over-hand across the floor towards Lena. He reached out and grabbed hold of Medved's jeans, feebly trying to drag the skinhead away. Medved looked down at him, his bloodied nose twitching with amusement.

'You don't give up, do you?' he said. 'Guess I'm *really* going to have to hurt you.'

He lifted his foot into the air, leaving it hovering above Alexei's head for a second. Then his boot came stamping down.

Missing Alexei by inches as he rolled out of the way. Grabbing the skinhead's leg, Alexei buried his teeth into Medved's calf like an animal. Medved howled with agony, stumbling into the heart monitor as he tried to shake Alexei off. Alexei let go and scuttled backwards, trying to block out the pain as he staggered to his feet.

Blinded by rage, Medved charged towards him and threw a wild haymaker in his direction. Alexei ducked out of the way, moving on sheer instinct. As the punch sailed over his head, ten years of kickboxing told Alexei that the skinhead had left himself exposed.

It was a split-second gap – no time to think. Alexei exploded upwards, channelling every ounce of muscle, every raging nerve-end into a soaring uppercut. All his years of pounding away at punchbags during training, of trading blows with opponents inside the ring, of winning and losing and picking himself off the canvas to fight again, seemed to meld into one glorious punch. He felt Medved's chin shudder as the uppercut connected. The impact of the blow knocked the skinhead off his feet: he was unconscious before he had hit the floor.

Alexei slumped down by the side of the hospital bed. His limbs were shaking, and his muscles felt utterly drained. Blood dripped down from his face, staining his clothes. Too exhausted to feel anything, he sat quietly, listening to the wail of police sirens as they approached the hospital.

Drawing on his aching muscles one last time, Alexei pulled himself up to Lena's bedside. A lock of hair had fallen across his girlfriend's face. Alexei gently tucked it behind her ear.

'You're safe now,' he whispered. 'No one will ever hurt you again.'

As he laid his head on her chest, Alexei felt Lena stir beneath him.

EPILOGUE: Old Friends

Secreted in the midst of a well-to-do area of Moscow, Patriarch's Ponds provided a serene retreat for its locals. Swans glided across the small lake, its waters rippling in the sunshine. It was a warm June day; the bitter snowfalls of winter now a distant memory. As the afternoon ripened into early evening, Muscovites escaped from their stuffy offices to stroll round the edge of the pond, and soak up the sun on the benches that lined the broad footpath. Lazy jazz music wafted over from a nearby cafe.

As the last of the afternoon's light began to fade, a young couple appeared. They were both in their late teens: a tall boy in jeans and a T-shirt, and a girl in a flowing summer dress. They walked slowly, tentatively, the boy glancing down with concern at his companion. Even though the top of the girl's head was swathed in thick white bandages, she still drew admiring glances from the men who passed by. Sheltering within the protective embrace of her boyfriend's arm, she didn't seem to notice.

'Are you OK?' Alexei asked. 'We can turn back if you're tired.'

Lena laughed softly. 'We haven't been here five minutes!'

'The doctor said you shouldn't be out for too long.'

'And he's just as big a fuss as you are.' She reached up and kissed Alexei on the cheek. 'Thank you, though. You have no idea how nice it is to breathe fresh air again. I thought I'd never get that hospital smell out of my nose!'

'Your parents will be pleased to hear you've been outside.'

'A little *too* pleased,' Lena replied solemnly. 'They want me to go back to Volgograd as soon as possible.'

'After everything that's happened, I can't blame them for that,' Alexei said. 'But what about you – what do you want to do?'

Lena sighed, and looked out across the pond. 'I don't know,' she admitted. 'The modelling's certainly out for a while. I don't think fashion photographers are all that keen on the bandaged look.'

'You're still the most beautiful girl I know,' Alexei said quietly.

Lena smiled, and squeezed his arm. 'Maybe I *should* go back to Volgograd,' she continued, 'but it doesn't feel right somehow . . . kind of like I'm running away. Does that sound crazy?'

'Not to me.'

'But you'd like to stay in Moscow, wouldn't you?'

Alexei shrugged. 'Maybe. I'd still like to study here one day. But right now, wherever you go, I'm going too.'

He had known that from the very second Lena had woken up. It was the only thing that Alexei was sure of any more. The previous eight weeks had been a crazed blur of activity. Having escaped down the hospital's back stairs moments before the police had arrived in Lena's room, Alexei had been relieved that his true identity had remained a secret. Although Rozalina Petrova's release had been splashed across the news reports and the papers, in her account of her ordeal the lawyer had never once mentioned his name, or that of Trojan Industries. The identity of the so-called 'Good Samaritans' who had saved her in Novodevichy Cemetery had remained a mystery, despite one tabloid offering a reward of 100,000 roubles if they stepped forward. Comforted by his anonymity, Alexei was able to attend the trials of Pavel, Medved and Marat – which had been fast-tracked due to the intense media glare surrounding their case. He concealed himself at the back of the gallery, watching with silent satisfaction as Rozalina provided a confident and damning testimony against the three men.

When the judge eventually handed down lengthy prison sentences, a piercing scream rent the gallery. Alexei looked across and saw Svetlana clutching at the guardrail.

'No!' she screamed. 'My baby! You bastards!'

Medved looked dolefully down at his feet as his girlfriend spat curses at the judge. Officers sprang forward to restrain her. As she was carried kicking and screaming from the courtroom, Svetlana's eyes met Alexei's. Hateful recognition flashed across her face before she was bundled outside.

For all her protestations to the contrary, Alexei could

see that Lena was starting to tire. He led her over to a bench and sat down beside her. A copy of the day's *Moscow Times* lay abandoned on the wooden slats, its pages rustling in the soft breeze. Its headline blazed 'BILLIONAIRE TYCOON ARRESTED'. The accompanying photograph showed Boris Lebedev being led out of the entrance of his Construktko building in handcuffs. Just as Darius Jordan had predicted, someone in the Moscow Eagles had implicated the tycoon. Apparently, the authorities had already frozen Lebedev's assets – Lilya was going to have to wait a while for a new fur coat. The *Moscow Times* was already eagerly anticipating Russia's 'Trial of the Century'.

As he sat in a comfortable silence with Lena, his arm around her shoulders, Alexei felt his skin tingle in warning. Glancing over his shoulder, he saw a slender figure watching them from the trees. It was Nadia.

Perhaps he should have been more surprised than he was. In a strange way, Alexei had expected to run into Nadia again. There had been a couple of times when he had thought about phoning her to check that she was OK, but somehow it hadn't seemed right. She must have felt the same, because she hadn't contacted him either.

Alexei got to his feet. 'I've just seen someone I've got to speak to,' he whispered to Lena. 'Don't run off anywhere.'

'Fat chance of that,' she grinned.

Alexei strode over to where Nadia was waiting, her hands clasped awkwardly in front of her. The blonde-haired girl's face was grave, and there were dark rings beneath her eyes. She smiled uncertainly as Alexei greeted her.

'Nadia! What are you doing here?'

'I was waiting outside the hospital for you. I wanted to talk to you but you came out with your girlfriend and I didn't want to intrude.'

'How are you? I haven't seen you since the night we freed Rozalina.'

'Not so good, I guess.' She paused. 'I'm under arrest.'

'What?' gasped Alexei. 'What for?'

'Marat told the police that I had uploaded the videos of the Eagles fighting on the net. Apparently once he started talking, he couldn't stop – he implicated anyone who'd even heard of the Eagles. They're going to charge me with abetting hate crimes. There's a good chance I'll end up in prison.'

'They can't do that!' Alexei protested. 'Without you, Rozalina would be dead! I'll tell the police that!'

Nadia smiled sadly. 'What will you tell them, Alexei? That I helped your secret gang-busting organization stop my brother? Marat tried to implicate you, but when the police couldn't track you down they thought he was making it up. And they won't believe you either – they'll think you're making it up to get the reward for saving Rozalina.'

'But it's just so unfair! How were you supposed to say no to Viktor?'

'I don't know,' Nadia said softly. 'But I should have found a way. My brother's gone now, and I want to make a fresh start. But I'll never be able to move on if I don't pay the price for what I did for the Eagles.' She paused.

'I haven't slept properly since Viktor killed himself. Maybe when I'm in prison . . .'

'I don't understand,' Alexei said, with a frown. 'If you're under arrest, how come you're out here?'

Nadia nodded behind her. Peering through the trees, Alexei noticed a man in a suit standing unobtrusively over by a set of railings.

'Police escort,' she said. 'I promised them more information if they let me say goodbye to an old friend.'

She looked away, biting her lip.

'Nadia . . .' Alexei began hesitantly. 'Whatever happens, I won't let you face it alone. Even if you do go to prison, I'll come and visit you as often as I can.'

Nadia shook her head. 'Your girlfriend is waiting for you. She needs you more than I do. Goodbye, Alexei.'

She turned and walked away without looking back. With a slight shake of the head, Alexei returned to the bench, where Lena was shielding her eyes from the sunlight as she observed his approach. 'Pretty girl,' she remarked. 'Friend of yours?'

Alexei watched as the man in the suit escorted Nadia away from the pond and helped her into the back of a white, unmarked car.

'Used to be,' he said.

'I hope you haven't been playing around behind my back,' Lena said, with mock-seriousness.

'Never,' Alexei replied, kissing her on the forehead. 'Come on. Let's get back to the hospital. I promised Uncle Stepan I'd cook for him tonight, and he gets grouchy if his dinner is late.'

As she got to her feet, Lena caught Alexei glancing at the newspaper headline. She gave him a shrewd look. 'Why do I get the funny feeling that something's gone on that you're not telling me about?'

'Female intuition?' teased Alexei.

A thoughtful look passed over Lena's face. 'I remember when I woke up . . .' she murmured, 'when I first saw you again . . . your face was bloodied and bruised. It looked like you'd been fighting. Did you get beaten up in the ring again?'

'I got knocked down a few times,' Alexei replied, gently squeezing Lena's side as they walked away through the waning sunshine. 'But I won in the end.'

WANT MORE?

Read on for an extract from

1. Dead Baby

A storm was coming.

Dark clouds rolled in towards Rio de Janeiro, looming above the luxury high-rise apartments and the hillside shanty towns alike. The atmosphere was taut with the threat of rain. On top of Corcovado mountain, the giant statue of Jesus that looked over the city had its arms outstretched, as though helpless in the face of the oncoming storm. Down on the beaches of Copacabana and Ipanema, glamorous bathers glanced up at the darkening sky and began pulling on T-shirts over their bikinis and swimming trunks. Raucous games of beach football came to a ragged end as players ran for shelter.

As the first spots of rain began to fall, Vitor 'Nene' Barbosa boarded a bus down by the beachfront, a basketball nestling under his arm. He was dressed in a tracksuit and his cropped black hair was still damp from his post-training shower. As he moved along the aisle towards the back of the bus, the driver called out a cheery greeting. Even though Nene had only just turned sixteen, everybody in Rio knew him – a basketball prodigy, he was destined for great things.

His nickname meant Baby – a joke, seeing as how Nene

had towered over his friends since he was a child. Now more than two metres tall, he was still growing. Nene played centre for Flamengo Petrobras, Rio's basketball team. The pivotal position on court, centres operated in and around the basket, where the rough-and-tumble demanded a muscular, athletic presence. You didn't normally play there at sixteen. But then normal rules didn't apply to Nene.

It wasn't only his height that made him special. The first time Nene had walked out on to the basketball court, his trainers squeaking on the hardwood surface, it felt as though he had come home. Things just made sense to him there. While his opponents tried to barge and muscle their way to the basket, Nene glided, snatching rebounds and sinking fade-aways as though the opposition wasn't even there. From the tip-off to the final buzzer, to him games felt like long, beautiful dreams.

Thirty points against Flamengo's rivals Brasilia in the last game – when Nene had been almost unplayable – had increased the hype surrounding him to fever pitch. Now there was talk of a call-up to the national team, even rumours that American scouts from the NBA were going to travel all the way down to Brazil to watch him. Nene had spent years gazing at the basketball posters that plastered his bedroom walls, dreaming of becoming the next Kobe Bryant. The thought that he might one day play on the same court as him made Nene dizzy with excitement.

It was about more than sporting glory, though. Everyone knew that there was serious money to be made in America, million-dollar contracts up for grabs. To Nene, who lived with his mother and two brothers in a small house in Rocinha – the largest *favela*, or shanty town, in Rio – such riches seemed unimaginable. Money was tight at the best of times, but recently Nene's mother had been laid up ill in bed, and the money Nene received for playing basketball and working in a supermarket was barely putting food on the table. If he could only impress an NBA scout, Nene told himself, then none of his family would have to worry about money ever again.

The bus driver honked his horn angrily, interrupting Nene's train of thought. There was a squeal of brakes and the bus came to an abrupt halt.

It was raining heavily now, large drops drumming against the windows. Peering outside, Nene saw that they had stopped at a quiet intersection on the edge of the Zona Sul, Rio's affluent tourist district. A group of teenagers had fanned out across the middle of the road, blocking the bus's path. They were dressed identically, in all-black T-shirts and knee-length shorts. His heart sinking, Nene saw that they were carrying guns: a deadly combination of pistols and semi-automatic rifles. The bus was being hijacked.

Perhaps he should have been more surprised – but then, gangs were a part of Rio's life as much as the beaches and the *Carnaval*. Made up predominantly of teenage boys, they maintained their own distinct identities and colours, marking out their territories in the *favelas* with lurid graffiti. Most of the time the gangs stayed on their own turf, concentrating on drug dealing and warring with their rivals. On the rare occasions that they ventured out en masse into downtown Rio, chaos ensued: robberies, rioting, even shoot-outs with the police.

Growing up in Rocinha, Nene knew all about infamous Rio gangs such as the Compadres and Quarto Comando. But the Compadres' colours were red and Quarto Comando's green; they wouldn't dress in all black like these guys. He forced himself to stay calm. Sports stars were cherished in Rio – even among the *favela* gangs. They weren't about to shoot holes into a *carioca*, a local boy, who had made good. He just had to keep quiet and do as he was told.

A dark-skinned boy in orange-tinted Ray-Bans stepped to the head of the gang and gestured at the bus driver to open the door. Then they strutted aboard the bus, their confidence bolstered by the firearms at their sides.

'We're the Comando Negro,' the boy with the sunglasses called out confidently. 'Get your money out now. Any trouble and we'll start firing.'

Immediately the passengers began rooting through their pockets and handbags, removing watches and jewellery in their eagerness to cooperate. Nene pulled out his wallet, careful not to make any sudden movements. He had never heard of the Comando Negro before and new gangs always spelled trouble – with everything to prove, and reputations to build, they tended to have twitchy trigger fingers.

The gang moved down the aisle, shouting at the passengers to throw their valuables into sports bags. One boy remained at the door of the bus, scanning the road for signs of the police. Whoever these guys were, Nene thought to himself, they looked pretty professional for a new outfit.

A black teenager with bleached-blond hair and a deep facial scar stopped by Nene's seat, his wide pupils and trembling hands bearing the hallmarks of heavy cocaine use. As the boy pointed at his open sports bag with a snub-nosed pistol, Nene tossed in his wallet, aware that he was throwing his family's dinner away with it.

Once the passengers had been stripped of their money, the gang filed quickly back off the bus. It had been a lightning raid. The blond-haired boy made to follow them, then turned back to Nene.

'I know you,' he said. 'Basketball player, aren't you?'

Nene nodded.

'We played against your team a couple of years back.'

'Yeah?'

'Yeah.' The boy nodded. 'You scored a lot of points that day. Didn't make me look so good.'

Nene shrugged. 'Didn't mean anything by it. All in the game, you know?'

The blond boy replied by cocking the hammer of his pistol and pressing it into the side of Nene's head. The metal barrel felt icy cold on his skin.

'You don't look so big now,' said the boy.

'I don't want any trouble,' Nene replied softly, his pulse racing. 'You've had my wallet. I haven't got anything else.'

The boy dug the barrel deeper into Nene's skin, forcing his head back against the window. He smiled coldly.

A whistle came from the front of the bus.

'Stripe!' the boy with the orange Ray-Bans called out. 'Angel said no pissing about, remember? If you've got his wallet, let's get the hell out of here.'

Stripe shot an angry glare at the other boy and then pulled the gun away from Nene's head.

'Next time,' he said.

As the boy walked away, Nene's shoulders slumped with relief. Looking down at his hands, he saw that they were shaking uncontrollably.

As the Comando Negro hurried off the bus and towards their 50cc motorbikes on the corner of the intersection, the sound of sirens struck up an insistent wail in the background. Joker – the boy with the orange Ray-Bans – smiled. It was going like clockwork, just as Angel had said it would. The passengers had handed over their valuables without a murmur. These beachfront people were all the same: soft.

He was about to speed away on his motorbike when he saw that Stripe had stopped in his tracks, a thoughtful look on his face.

'Come on, Stripe! We're done!'

The blond-haired boy ignored him. Turning abruptly on his heel, he walked back through the rain towards the bus.

'Where the hell are you going now?' Joker called out. 'The police'll be here soon!'

Deep in his heart, however, he knew exactly where Stripe was going – Joker had known him long enough for that. Perhaps Angel could have stopped him, but then Angel wasn't here. All Joker could do was watch, revving his bike engine in frustration. Through the bus windows he saw Stripe reboard the vehicle and stride back along the aisle towards the tall boy with the basketball. Stripe said something, raising his gun.

There was a loud popping sound and then a spray of red liquid splattered against the window where the basketballer's head had been a moment beforehand.

As a chorus of horrified screams went up from the bus's passengers, Stripe walked nonchalantly back down the steps and towards Joker.

'What?' he said, catching Joker's sideways glance. 'He made me look bad.'

Kicking his motorbike into life, Stripe drove quickly away down a side street. Joker swore loudly and gestured for the rest of the Comando Negro to follow suit. They sped off in an angry whine of engines, leaving the bus stationary in the middle of the road, the rain beginning to collect in puddles around it.

2. Blood Relative

The children filed out of Sacred Heart School amid riotous laughter, relieved to have escaped for another day. To Luiz Alves, who was walking quickly through the jostling crowds, the loud shouts and giggles sounded like a chorus of zoo animals. Fifteen years old, with light-brown skin, curly black hair and broad shoulders that filled out his white school shirt, Luiz moved with a quiet self-assurance that suggested he didn't mind being on his own.

Sacred Heart was a private school set in the heart of Botafogo, a bustling, middle-class neighbourhood of Rio, where the streets were dotted with cafes, museums and bookshops. With the school charging expensive fees, the pupils were a mixture of foreign students and children from well-to-do local families. English was the language heard in the corridors and the classrooms, not Brazilian Portuguese. While Sacred Heart could boast state-of-the-art computer rooms and sports facilities, the security cameras at the school exits and the high iron railings provided a constant reminder that not everywhere in Rio was as affluent, or as safe.

As Luiz walked away down the street, a football flew past his ear and he heard a familiar voice cry out, 'Hey, asshole!'

He turned to see his friend Gui standing by the gates, his arm draped over the shoulder of a pretty blonde girl. 'We're going down to the beach,' he called out. 'You coming?'

Luiz shook his head. 'It's Ana's birthday,' he shouted back. 'I've got to go home.'

Gui shrugged. 'Your loss, asshole! See you tomorrow.'

With a wave, Luiz turned away. As he walked off, he heard Gui's girl scream with laughter. Ordinarily Luiz wouldn't have thought twice about going with them, but today was different. His younger sister, Ana, was turning fourteen and he wanted to be home when she got back from school. Their foster parents, Francesco and Mariella, were in São Paulo for two weeks, researching an exclusive story for *O Globo*, the newspaper they both worked for. When they returned, the family was going out for a special meal in one of the posh restaurants in the Zona Sul, but for tonight it was going to be just Luiz and Ana.

Life hadn't always been so comfortable. Luiz and Ana had grown up in very different surroundings, in the sprawling *favela* of Santa Marta that clung to the hillside overlooking Botafogo. Abandoned by their dad after Ana's birth, they were brought up by their mum on her own. When she succumbed to cancer, a local priest had come to the rescue, taking Luiz and Ana in and contacting an adoption agency. A week later, Francesco and Mariella had arrived to collect them from the mission, and had then introduced them to their new home in Botafogo.

Settling in hadn't been easy. On Luiz's first day at Sacred Heart, one of the kids had made the mistake of laughing at his coarse *favela* accent. It had taken three teachers to prise Luiz off him and the other boy had had to go to hospital. Luiz had nearly been expelled on his very first day; after that, the other pupils gave him a wide, wary berth, as if he were a dangerous animal or a leper. In the end it had been Gui – irrepressible, fun-loving Gui – who had plonked himself down next to Luiz during a maths lesson and started cracking jokes. They had been best friends ever since.

Gradually Luiz had begun to feel more at home. He managed to rein in his temper and stopped taking offence at every perceived slight. It had been two years since he had last been in a fight – Ana joked that he was turning into a pacifist. Luiz knew that his anger would never entirely disappear, though, that it bubbled somewhere deep within his soul. Nor had he forgotten about Santa Marta. For all the dangers of the *favela*, Luiz missed its vibrancy, the energy that crackled through the streets. He wasn't stupid – he knew what his life would be like if he was still up there. He'd probably be in one of the gangs, selling drugs. There were only so many ways you could make money in the *favelas*, especially without parents, and you had to eat. Even so, walking underneath the shadow of Santa Marta every day, it was hard not to feel the occasional pang of regret.

Shielding his eyes from the sun, Luiz looked up the hillside at the cramped dwellings piled on top of one another, at the makeshift buildings with their slanting roofs and the winding, treacherously narrow alleyways. A long time had passed since he had last been back to Santa Marta – four years, maybe. At first he had cut school to sneak up to the *favela*, meeting with his old friends and laughing about his new life. Eventually, tired of the arguments caused by Luiz slipping out, Ana had made him promise not to go back. She had a habit of making Luiz do things he didn't want to. Little sisters were like that, he grumbled to himself.

If Luiz had taken time to come to terms with their new life, Ana had fitted in seamlessly. Bubbly and popular, she had quickly caught up with her schoolwork and was soon outstripping her classmates. Earlier that very year, she had won the lead in the school play. Watching Ana up on the stage, Luiz felt he would burst with pride.

Now his sister had set her heart on becoming a journalist like their foster parents and was getting work experience at *O Globo*. In the last few weeks, Ana had been spending increasing amounts of time researching a piece she was hoping to show the editors at the newspaper. No matter how much Luiz teased her about her big 'scoop', she refused to talk about it. It was typical Ana – when she had her heart set on something, she went out and got it. Unlike her brother. God only knew what Luiz was going to do when he left school. He could just about keep up in class but was no rocket scientist – as Gui was quick to point out.

Luiz shook his head. Missing the beach for his sister's birthday was one thing, but his best friend would piss himself laughing if he could see Luiz pondering such deep thoughts.

Home was a detached house down a quiet residential street. As he turned the key in the front door, Luiz wasn't surprised to find that he had got back before Ana. He flicked on the television, then began rooting around in the fridge for something to eat. The news was still showing footage of the bus that had been held up two days ago, the camera focusing on the bloodstained window where Nene Barbosa had been killed. Something about this murder – the sheer senselessness of it – seemed to have shocked the city. Luiz could understand that. Only a month ago, he had watched Nene playing basketball for Flamengo, marvelling at the fact that the boy was only a year older than him. And now someone had shot him in the head.

The camera cut to a press conference on the steps of a police station. A bulky man in an expensive suit was standing in front of a bank of microphones, sweat glistening on top of his bald head.

'Councillor Cruz,' one of the reporters called out, 'I've been told that the police suspect the Barbosa murder was the work of the same gang responsible for the looting of the jewellery store in Ipanema – a gang calling themselves the Comando Negro. Can you confirm or deny these reports?'

The bald man held up his hands. 'The police are still carrying out their investigations and I'm not prepared to comment directly yet. What I will say is that – whatever name they call themselves – this pack of *favela* hoodlums has extinguished the life of one of Rio's most promising young men. Be assured that I will not rest until the animals responsible are in prison.'

Luiz shook his head. Councillor Jorge Cruz was always on the television bad-mouthing the *favelas*. He made it sound as though everyone who lived in the shanty towns was a member of a gang. Luiz's foster parents reckoned that there was something fishy about Cruz himself – his dad had investigated several shady business deals that had the councillor's fingerprints on them but could never prove anything. Not everyone in Rio had such a bad opinion of the *favelas*, but idiots like Cruz didn't help matters.

Luiz changed the channel to MTV and slumped down on the couch with a sandwich. He was dozing through an R&B video when he heard the front door open. Finally, Ana was back.

'You took your time,' he called out. 'You're late for your own party!'

'No one said anything about a party,' a man's voice replied.

Luiz sprang up from the sofa as three strangers walked casually into the room. Dressed in business suits, they carried themselves with the calm self-confidence of policemen. None of them bothered to flash any ID cards, however, and they had just walked uninvited into Luiz's house.

'Who are you?' he said.

'Nice place,' one of the men said conversationally, ignoring the question.

Shorter than his two companions, he was wearing dark sunglasses. He picked up a vase Luiz's mum had brought back from a trip to Europe and inspected it curiously.

'What do you want?' Luiz asked, his heart beating loudly.

'Just a chat. Nothing to get excited about,' the man replied. He glanced around the room. 'Perhaps here isn't the best place, though.'

'I can't go anywhere,' Luiz said, stalling. 'My sister's gone to the shops and she hasn't got a key.'

The man glanced up sharply and put down the vase. 'That's not a good start,' he said. 'All we want is a chat and already you're lying to us. Ana's not at the shops. What you should be asking yourself, Luiz, is – where is she?'

He knew their names. Luiz's blood froze.

'What do you mean, where is she? Is Ana all right? What have you done with her?'

'Such a lot of questions!' the man said, smiling. 'Why don't you come with us and we'll talk about it?'

'I'm not going anywhere until you tell me where Ana is,' Luiz replied stubbornly.

One of the other men clamped a hand down on Luiz's arm.

'Get moving, you little shit,' he said.

Luiz didn't even think about it. Instinctively he swung his left elbow into the man's face, felt his nose crumple on impact. The man cried out and staggered back, clutching his face. Immediately Luiz was on his toes, vaulting over the couch as the man with the sunglasses leaned over to grab him. As the third man raced to cut off the doorway, Luiz kicked him hard in the kneecap. He was rewarded by a loud curse and a clumsy punch thrown in his direction. Stepping neatly out of the way, Luiz caught the man on the side of the head with a punch of his own and watched him drop to the floor. Then he whirled round to take on his final assailant.

Too late.

The man with the sunglasses was standing right behind

him, a black taser in his hand. He pressed the trigger, firing two darts through Luiz's clothes and into his skin. A sheet of white pain enveloped Luiz, and he screamed in agony as he fell to the floor. As he lay there, limbs trembling, unable to fight back, the man produced a cloth from his pocket and pressed it over Luiz's face. For a second he was overwhelmed by a sickly sweet smell and then everything went black.